MARCHESE'S
FORGOTTEN
BRIDE

MARCHESE'S FORGOTTEN BRIDE

BY

MICHELLE REID

First published in Great Britain 2009
Large Print edition 2010
Harlequin Mills & Boon Limited,
Eton House, 18-24 Paradise Road,
Richmond, Surrey TW9 1SR

© Michelle Reid 2009

ISBN: 978 0 263 21172 6

Harlequin Mills & Boon policy is to use papers that are
natural, renewable and recyclable products and made
from wood grown in sustainable forests. The logging and
manufacturing process conform to the legal environmental
regulations of the country of origin.

Printed and bound in Great Britain
by CPI Antony Rowe, Chippenham, Wiltshire

CHAPTER ONE

THE restaurant bar had become so crowded that Cassie discovered it was a struggle to lift her glass to her lips. Not that she minded standing there, soaking up the bright, noisy atmosphere, she told herself, eyes busily taking in the sight of her fellow workmates all dressed up in their best party glamour for this evening's introductory treat laid on by their new boss.

It had been so long since she'd been to anything like this and it felt so good to be here. She'd even indulged in a frighteningly expensive new dress for herself, made of a smooth black-on-charcoal embossed silk, which skimmed her slender figure and felt fabulously stylish and chic. With her hair professionally cut and styled for the first time in years, now her pale golden locks felt wonderful as they brushed against her naked shoulders whenever she moved her head.

'Your eyes are sparkling like big shiny emeralds,' Ella remarked dryly beside her. 'You're loving this, aren't you?'

A brilliant smile enhanced the shape of Cassie's rose-glossed mouth. 'I'd forgotten what it's like to actually enjoy being a part of such a noisy, mad crush!'

'Well, here's to a lot more of the same now the twins are a bit older.' Ella somehow managed to lift her glass high enough to chink it against Cassie's. 'No more skimping and saving and emulating an overworked drudge now you don't need to pay those crazy pre-school nursery fees.'

'From single working mum to wild party girl in one leap.' Cassie laughed. 'Do you want me to do a bit of husband hunting at the same time?'

'God, no.' Ella shuddered and Cassie watched a cloud settle across her friend's pretty face.

Ella was fresh out of a long-term relationship with a guy who'd dumped her six weeks away from their wedding day with the classic—I'm just not ready to be tied down—excuse. Cassie knew exactly what that felt like—the dumping part anyway. Only in her case she'd been left pregnant with twins.

'He's history, Ella,' she reminded her firmly, 'forget about him.'

With a blink of her long black eyelashes Ella nodded, setting her bobbed dark hair swinging around her face. 'Yes, I've moved on, haven't I?'

Haven't we both? Cassie thought. 'With bells on,' she agreed and gave their glasses a second chink. 'Think huge great bodybuilder with the temperament of a pussycat instead of razor-sharp share-dealer with the genetic make-up of a slithery snake.'

Ella burst out laughing at the comparison between her current lover and the one that had got away. The sound of her laughter caught the attention of several people crushed in around them and with a shift of bodies their conversation changed to include those around them. The next few minutes went by with the easy camaraderie that came from people who worked in close proximity five days a week, and the party atmosphere moved up a gear with the help of the free-flowing wine. The crush tightened then eased and tightened again as people began to circulate.

'When are they going to start herding us upstairs to eat?' Ella sighed a while later. 'I'm starving.'

'I think we must be waiting for the new boss to arrive,' Cassie said, squeezing a sip of wine from her glass.

'Well, if it gets any more crowded in here we'll be like sardines in a can,' her friend complained, 'although I wouldn't mind playing sardines with the guy that's just walked in here with our MD and a clutch of scary bigwig types…'

Turning her head to look in the direction that Ella was looking, Cassie just wasn't prepared for what came next. Shock struck her blindside. For the next few horrible seconds she felt as if she were falling off the edge of a cliff! Her legs went hollow beneath her then started to fill up again from her toes with a tingling wild rush of hot static as instant recognition screamed through her head. She had not laid eyes on him in six long years, yet each lean, hard, vital inch of him battered her senses with a familiarity that dragged her heart to a shuddering stop.

And who could miss him? she thought helplessly as her heart lurched into action again with a blunt, hammering beat. He was so tall he stood a good head and shoulders above the others clustered around him, even with his dark head tilted down a little so he could hear what their short and portly MD was saying over the noisy buzz of conversation filling up the bar. Yet Cassie knew the top of that head; she knew it so intimately it could have been only an hour ago that she'd run her fingers through the thick layers of vibrant black silk. Her fingers even twitched tautly around her wineglass in stinging recognition, almost sending the glass and its contents crashing to the white marble floor beneath her strappy black mules.

'Methinks we are getting our first eyeful of our new boss,' Ella murmured beside her, 'and just feel the change to the buzz in here...'

It took Cassie several seconds to absorb that piece of information because she was too busy trying to deal with the buzz going on inside herself.

'No,' she managed with a shivery cold whisper, 'that isn't him.'

'Are you sure...?' Ella took a moment to reassess the man in question, while all Cassie could do was to stand there, locked in her own private form of hell. Then, 'No, it's got to be him, Cassie,' her friend determined. 'That totally gorgeous piece of manhood just can't go by any other name than the oh-so-sexy-sounding Alessandro Marchese.'

The name rolled off Ella's tongue like a sensual fantasy. Cassie suffered a stinging, sharp jolt to her chest. Alessandro Marchese? Was Ella looking at a different man?

'You mark my words, we are looking at a few billion dollars of hot Italian breeding standing over there, *cara,*' Ella mocked dryly, 'and, if I'm not mistaken, the lady in red clinging to his arm can match him gene for superior gene...'

The lady in red...

Wrenching her gaze sideways, Cassie confirmed that indeed she and Ella were looking at the same man as she stared at the fabulously beautiful, glossy black-haired creature wearing an exquisitely cut blood-red dress who was clinging to his arm while she listened to what the two men were saying. They looked at ease with each other—intimate—like two lovers who'd been lovers for a very long time.

And Ella was right, they did suit each other—in the same way that the name *Alessandro Marchese* suited him far better than the plain *Sandro Rossi* Cassie had known him by did!

As she dragged her eyes back to him, a burning, sick bitterness dried up her throat when she discovered that he'd lifted his head up and she was now getting a full-on view of his face— a face that had lost none of its raw masculine impact in the six years since she'd last looked at it, she acknowledged painfully. Those long, lazy eyelids, the straight, fleshless nose, the slender and firm yet shatteringly sensual mouth... Like someone harbouring a death wish, Cassie drank in the smooth stretch of gold skin across his stunning high cheekbones and the way his lavishly long and thick black eyelashes almost brushed against those stunning cheekbones as he turned a wry, sexy smile on the woman in the red dress.

If she'd had the strength in her legs she would be walking over there to slap that smile off his lying face! Alessandro Marchese... Who was he trying to kid? Was he a crook or something that he had to use an assumed name these days? Or was she the one who'd been lied to? The one who'd been sucked in by his fabulous dark looks and his gorgeously intense sincerity, the one who'd been so skilfully romanced and thoroughly seduced then left like an unwanted breakfast when he'd swanned off back to his native Italy to get on with his real life?

The sting of betrayal stalked down her backbone like taunting fingers as she studied the way he was standing there exuding the supremely relaxed self-assurance which came automatically to smooth-tongued, sexually confident brutes. Cassie hated him yet she could not stop herself from feasting on him, couldn't stop her eyes from sliding down the column of his strong, bronzed throat to the width of his broad shoulders set inside a superbly crafted dark lounge suit, and across the white shirt that did absolutely nothing to subdue the hard-muscled power in his long, lean physique.

And she remembered it all, every intimate detail, from the hair-roughened power of his rich golden torso, with its satin-tight abdomen that felt like warm, living satin to touch, and the sleek, corded sinew which angled so dramatically down the narrow bowl of his hips to the—

She had to get out of here—

The need struck with a startling punch of delayed reaction that sent her slender body jerking up straight. As if he picked up the violence in her reaction, he lifted those heavy eyelids and looked directly into her face, forcing her into a head-on collision with a pair of piercingly deep-set blacker-than-black eyes that she'd wished, hoped, prayed she would never have to look into again!

Time suddenly ground to a shimmering standstill. The bright, noisy chatter filling the bar just stopped as if someone had thrown up a glass wall, shutting the two of them off from everyone else as six long years of grimly burying his memory shattered in the wild rush of images that began to rampage around her head.

Sandro laughing…Sandro smiling that dryly amused smile when she'd shyly tried to flirt with him…Sandro holding her…kissing her…Sandro oh, so gentle then turning hot and fierce and devouringly intense as they made love.

A shaft of pure sexual fire stroked right down her middle, catching Cassie out so badly she sucked in her breath. The breath forced her lips apart and made his fabulous eyelashes flicker as he honed his attention on to her mouth, and her whole body stung and tightened in direct response to that luminous dark glance. She didn't want to feel like this. She wanted to be left cold by the sight of him and she was appalled that that was not how it was!

Like a man slowly tracking old pleasures, he lifted his gaze to take in the waterfall shine of her pale gold hair brushing against her trembling white shoulders, then dropped to where the strapless structure of her dress hugged the creamy thrust of her breasts. The message powering out of his eyes was so hot and so ele-mentally sexual Cassie felt a terrible flush of agonised awareness prickle her fair skin. She wanted to cry out in shrill, pained, angry protest but she couldn't. She had never felt so agonis-ingly exposed to her own wretched weakness in her entire life.

It did not occur to her that it had taken him this long to recognise her, until he finally lifted his eyes back to her eyes and she watched his lazy, searching expression alter to a look of shock. For the next few taut seconds she actually thought he was going to keel over, the way his eyes widened then turned as black as Hades and his face drained of its beautiful bronzed tan. She stopped breathing—she stopped doing anything—breathing, hearing, thinking…

Then he stiffened his long body up and abruptly turned his back on her, blanking her out with a cruel, ruthless economy that was like having a door slammed in her face.

Again.

Left totally, utterly stunned and shaken by the sheer brutality of his rejection, Cassie thought that she was the one going to faint. Someone accidentally knocked her arm, almost spilling her drink, but she barely noticed. Someone else spoke to her but she couldn't work out a single word that they said. She knew she'd gone pale because she *felt* pale; a clammy kind of chill had settled over her flesh. And worse—much worse—was the way an already badly wounded part of her was cracking open like a fissure forming a fresh wound over a jagged old one in recognition that he could still do that to her after all of these years and here of all places, in full view of all her work colleagues.

Somehow—she didn't really know how—she managed to turn away from him. She managed to draw in a few shallow breaths. She was feeling so badly shaken up inside it took all her control not to start moving like a battering ram in her desperation to get out of the now suffocating crush.

'Do you think they'll let us go and eat now?' she heard Ella murmur wistfully.

And it came as a further shock to realise that the whole shattering incident must have only lasted a few seconds. 'Yes,' she breathed like a metal-encased robot set on automation.

Who was she…?

The question lit up Alessandro's brain like a bolt of lightning and sent a too-familiar pain whipping across the front of his head, forcing him to lift a hand up to rub at his brow.

And he felt weird, as if something was scooping him out from the inside.

Could instant sexual attraction be so strong it could threaten to take the legs from beneath you? he wondered. It was years—he couldn't remember the last time the sight of a beautiful woman had felled him so completely as the blonde had just done. And he was angry with himself for letting it happen here of all places, with a woman who'd just become one of the newest members of his international workforce. It was unprofessional—and damned inconvenient when he—

'Headache, Alessandro?' Always aware of any change in his mood, Pandora spoke, her voice reaching him softly laced with concern.

'No.' Dropping the hand from his face, he found himself turning to narrow another look at the blonde.

Even her rear view sent that same instant shaft of fire burning through him, almost knocking him sideways with its power. And her hair—her hair…there was something about the colour of her hair and the way it caressed her slender white shoulders—

'You've gone a worrying shade of pale, *cara,*' Pandora persisted. 'Are you sure you—?'

'Jet lag,' he dismissed with irritation, most of his attention still fixed on the blonde. 'We have just arrived here straight off a fifteen-hour flight. Don't fuss, Pandora. You know it annoys the hell out of me.'

Who was she…? And why was he getting this

gut-shaking feeling that he had seen her somewhere before…?

'And you worked instead of resting…' His companion ignored his warning. 'One day, Alessandro, you will—'

Beside him, Jason Farrow suddenly clapped his hands together, drowning out the rest of what Pandora was saying and making Alessandro fight the need to wince as the unwelcome sound crashed through his aching head.

'Ladies and gentlemen, may I please have your attention?' the current MD of BarTec prompted, causing silence to fold around the room as everyone looked expectantly in their direction.

Grimly trying to shake off the strange sensations running through him, Alessandro took in the full impact of a hundred pairs of eyes honed exclusively on him.

He knew her. The more he thought about it the more sure he became that he'd met her somewhere before. Her pale golden hair, her luminous green eyes, her full, soft, sexy pink mouth… He tried not to frown as he tracked through his memory banks looking for clues as to how or where he knew her, with that weird, hollowing-out feeling increasing as he did…

Her gently moulded cheekbones and small, straight nose, her cute, slightly pointed chin…

He disentangled himself from Pandora's clinging hand, shocked suddenly by how appalled he felt to have her show such intimacy with him.

'Can I ask you all to offer a warm welcome to the new owner of BarTec, Alessandro Marchese…?'

Having been forced to turn around again, Cassie saw that Sandro—or whatever it was he called himself these days—was still frowning as if something had thoroughly ruined his day. Well, join the club, she thought as a flow of acid contempt for him thankfully cleared out her battered feelings of hurt and dismay. Who the heck did he think he was that he felt he had the right to blank her as if she were nobody?

She listened to the second wave of applause ripple through the bar area, though she didn't bother to join in. She would rather cut off her hands than applaud this man. She hated him. Now that she was looking at him without the first incapacitating rush of shock cluttering up her emotions, she was remembering just how much she hated and despised Sandro Rossi—or, in this case, Alessandro Marchese.

'*Grazie molto per la vostra accoglienza calorosa...*' the man himself responded in a rich, deep, sensually delivered Italian which caused a collective gasp of delicious appreciation from the females present in the bar, while his beautiful companion touched his arm and murmured something to him that turned his frown to a grimace, then a short second later into a smile that clutched Cassie's stomach muscles in a vice-like grip and just captivated everyone else.

'My apologies,' he murmured, 'allow me to repeat that in English... Thank you very much for your warm welcome...'

'Oh, my,' Ella breathed beside Cassie. 'Now, that was very, very sexy indeed. Do you think he deliberately set out to disarm us all with the piece of theatre?'

Probably, Cassie thought cynically, fighting to keep her bitter feelings from showing on her face. In truth she was surprised the sharp-eyed Ella hadn't noticed what had been passing between her best friend and their new boss—surprised that the whole darn room hadn't noticed!

Sandro was now busy charming everyone as he mapped out his plans for the company, and he did it by conveying an air of smoothly polished self-assurance aimed to allay everyone's fears about their future at BarTec. Lowering her eyes, Cassie listened without really hearing, unwillingly tuned in to the flowing resonance of his voice but without catching more than the odd word because her mind was elsewhere, rolling back the years to a time when she'd first heard that voice.

It hadn't changed—*he* hadn't changed. Whatever he preferred to call himself these days, he was still the man who'd used those sexy dark base tones and his easy-going charm to make her fall in love with him before casting her aside once he'd enjoyed the pleasures of her body, leaving her desolate, pregnant and alone.

A second crash of applause woke her up with a shudder. Sandro had finished speaking and was now smiling down at the woman in the red dress. Cassie wanted to leave. It was horrible just how badly she wanted to just walk through that door and go. But Sandro was still blocking the exit along with his cluster of smartly dressed minions, who all looked as slick and as sharp as he did.

Could she squeeze past them without him noticing? Would he care that she was leaving if she did? The sizzle of temptation fizzed through her body alongside the angry bitterness already swimming through it.

'At last we get to be fed.' Ella's dry comment forced her to take note of the way everyone was beginning to make a move towards the stairs which led to the restaurant above, and grim common sense arrived as Cassie felt herself swept up in the general exodus.

She knew she could not afford the luxury of just walking out of here. She needed her job at BarTec. She did not need the rash of questions bound to fly at her if she did decide to go.

Tagging along beside Ella, she listened to her friend chattering away ten to the dozen about their gorgeously interesting new boss to those crowded around them while Cassie just felt completely shut off.

I don't know you. I don't want to know you. Please don't ring this number again...

Those cold words of rejection echoed around

her head. From fierce, dark, passionate lover to contemptuous stranger in the blink of an eyelash. To hell with the fact that he'd been her first lover, or that he'd left her pregnant and terrified and bewildered. Sandro had taught her the hardest way possible that men like him had no conscience whatsoever when it came to pursuing a woman they desired until they'd caught her, and no honour at all when it came to dumping them after their desire had been slaked.

CHAPTER TWO

CASSIE and Ella found themselves placed at the same table in the farthest corner of the restaurant along with the rest of their colleagues from the accounts department. The only stranger at the table was a very good-looking, smartly presented man who introduced himself as, 'Gio Rozario, one of Alessandro's team.'

The meal progressed through its different courses with everyone firing eager questions at him, which he fielded with friendly ease and a return volley of questions of his own. He seemed genuinely interested in all of them. He *charmed* them all the way his employer had done downstairs in the bar.

Barely touching her food, Cassie watched and listened and contributed very little. She'd already noted that each table had at least one team member sitting at it, and it didn't take many brain cells to work out that the seating had been intentionally arranged this way so the spies in their midst could gather in information and impressions about BarTec employees, which they were bound to feed back to their boss.

In other words, the Marchese mob was deep into work mode while the rest of them were off-duty and off-guard. Clever, she thought grudgingly. The wine was still flowing freely and she would be prepared to bet that by the time this evening was over few of them would walk out of here with many secrets intact.

Without her wanting them to do it, her eyes drifted across the room to the huge circular table set in the middle of the restaurant where her one major secret sat dining with the members of the board. He looked relaxed, like his team, in control of the conversation happening around him—a smooth and sophisticated corporate giant with the body of an athlete and the profile of a heartbreaker.

And he had the same vibrant dark hair and eyes as Anthony…

Oh, God—not bothering to fight the need to escape any longer, Cassie got to her feet.

'Excuse me,' she mumbled, 'I need to visit the ladies' room,' then she picked her up her evening purse and walked blindly towards the stairs.

Under cover of his half-lowered eyelids, Alessandro watched the slender blonde traverse the room towards the stairwell. She must be going to use the wash room which was situated downstairs in the bar area, he judged, tension singing along the corded sinew of his groin as he followed the sensual grace with which she moved.

This first full view he'd had of her without the crush blotting most of her out sent his gaze flowing down the delicate curves of her slim figure displayed inside the little grey and black dress she was wearing that did a lot to enhance the creamy smoothness of her skin. Fine-boned, he observed, slightly built with a nicely curving, neat behind and fabulous long legs with neat ankles elevated by the heels of her shiny black mules.

She started walking down the staircase, her silky, pale hair swinging forward as she bent her head to watch her footing on the shiny white marble steps, an elegant white hand reaching out to grasp the banister rail. Something stung across his front, like sensual fingernails scoring the hairs covering his chest, and once more the bolt of lightning shot through his head.

He frowned, having to fight the need to lift his hand up and rub at his aching brow again. At the bend in the staircase he saw her stop to fumble in her evening bag and watched her lift a mobile phone to her ear.

Who was it she wanted to talk to? A lover? A husband?

Lips flattening back against his teeth, he wished he knew why the prospect of either was having a gut-grinding effect on him.

'Cassie Janus,' Jason Farrow inserted smoothly beside him.

Forced to look in the other man's direction, Alessandro schooled his expression to reveal absolutely nothing but a mild question as to what it was the other man was talking about.

'I noticed your interest earlier,' the current MD confided as if it should earn him brownie points.

Sandro said nothing, though he was absolutely sure Jason Farrow had not said all that he wanted to say. And anyway, he was waiting to find out if the name *Cassie Janus* made some kind of connection in him.

It didn't.

'She heads our accounts team,' the older man supplied helpfully. 'Has a mind like a calculator, though you wouldn't think it to look at her, heh?'

Alessandro had been predisposed to dislike Jason Farrow before he'd even met him but that sexist remark tied it up for him. If Farrow had dared to add a conspiratorial wink Alessandro suspected he would have stood up and hit him.

A company the size of BarTec was small fry by comparison to the big fish he usually liked to bury his teeth into. However, the company had developed some ground-breaking technology in microelectronics he would much rather have safely caught under the Marchese umbrella than let his competitors get hold of it. So when Angus Barton decided to sell BarTec due to ill health, he'd jumped at the chance to buy him out. Angus was a close friend of his late father's. Even if he had not been interested in anything BarTec had to offer he would have lifted the load of responsibility from Angus's weary shoulders based on that long friendship alone. It was Angus who'd confessed he'd made some rash decisions during the months before he decided it was time to sell. Elevating Jason Farrow to the position of managing director had been one of those decisions. 'He's a self-opinionated bully. He certainly bullied me, anyway.' The sad grimace his father's old friend had offered up had not been a comfortable thing to behold because it had shown a man who knew he was losing the will to fight his many battles.

This evening had been arranged as a way of easing the troubled minds of those employees important to him, as to what he meant to do with the company, and to weed out those who were not going to make it beyond the scrutiny of his team. Jason Farrow was fast becoming the name at the top of that throw-away list. He looked what he was, a well-shod, well-fed, self-promoting dinosaur who dared to see power in voicing such observations to him. When he got to know him better, he would learn the hard way that it wasn't the case.

As it was… 'You have a problem with women in the working environment?' Alessandro prompted casually.

'God, no, they lighten my day!' Farrow declared with a nerve-needling grin. 'Though I still have to be convinced that women are capable of giving one hundred per cent to their careers, female hormones being what they are,' he confided. 'Cassie's situation makes her one of the luckier ones working at BarTec—she was Angus's little pet. Angus employed her when really she wasn't up to taking on the commitment required of her. Still—' Farrow shrugged, unaware that Sandro's eyes had lowered and narrowed as he bit back the desire to question Farrow further as to what stopped Cassie Janus from giving her full commitment to her job. 'That's what you get when you let personal feelings get in the way of good business sense,' BarTec's managing director continued in a slightly peevish tone. 'I had a much better candidate lined up for Cassie's job but Angus knew her late father, so…'

Behind his lowered eyelids Alessandro's brain shut out the rest of what Farrow was saying when his instincts suddenly sharpened on what he saw as a link between himself and the woman who'd managed to knock his senses for six.

Angus… Had he met her during one of his weekend stays with Angus Barton?

'You of all people must agree that there is no place in business for sentimentality,' he tuned back in to catch. 'She's easy on the eyes, as you've already noticed, but a pretty face and figure can be a distraction best kept out of the office, in my opinion.'

Alessandro had heard enough. 'Pandora...' he drawled to catch the attention of the member of his team sharing this table with him.

Pandora Batiste turned her glossy dark head and smiled the kind of naturally sensual smile that had the power to blow most men's libido to bits.

'Tell Mr Farrow what you do to earn the outrageous annual salary I pay to you,' Alessandro urged casually.

Pandora laughed. 'Outrageous indeed. I earn every euro and you know it, Alessandro,' she scolded him, then turned her drop-dead smile on Jason Farrow. 'As from Monday morning you and I will be working closely together to make my transition into Angus Barton's venerable shoes as painless for everyone as we can possibly make it, Mr Farrow,' she enlightened. 'I hope I can rely on your loyalty and support...'

The message was as clear as the ruddy hue

that flooded into Jason Farrow's face. He was about to find out the tough way that there was indeed no room for sentimentality or distraction in business with the beautiful Pandora around to pull rank on him.

Alessandro picked up his barely touched glass of wine and rose to his feet. 'If you will excuse me, it's time for me to circulate,' he murmured smoothly and strode off, grimly satisfied Farrow had received a mental kick in the teeth in return for his sexist remarks and for bullying Angus.

Angus… His frown came back as he crossed the stairwell, aware that his feet wanted to take him down those stairs to confront Cassie Janus about his suspicion that they'd met before but even more aware that with Farrow's eyes burning a hole in his back he could not afford to be seen to be singling her out.

She was a distraction, he acknowledged, if only to himself. And why did Farrow believe he had a right to question her commitment to the company? Was this a case of another rash decision Angus had made as his illness began to take hold?

Cassie was standing in the now-empty bar area with her eyes closed as she listened to the soothing voice Jenny, her next-door neighbour, was using to reassure her that the twins were OK. 'All tucked up in bed and fast asleep,' Jenny told her. 'They've been absolute angels. You should let me do this for you more often, Cassie. It's a real treat for me to play granny when my own grandchildren are so far away. And I have to admit,' she added with a chuckle, 'it's lovely to be able to watch anything I like on television other than Larry's endless football.'

The *angels* had been angels because Cassie had witnessed the deal being struck between them and Jenny when they thought she wasn't paying attention. Having eagerly presented Jenny with a box of chocolates, the twins had then gone into a dance of miming appeals which translated as 'Just one chocolate each without Mummy knowing and we'll go to bed when you say'. Jenny had played along with them, of course, and of course Cassie had let them get away with it. She now had this cosy image of her next-door neighbour stretched out in the stuffed old armchair in front of the TV set with her shoes off and her feet resting on top of the old coffee table while the box of half-ravaged chocolates rested conveniently on her lap.

'So what did you decide to watch?' she asked, feeling a smile relax some of the tension from her mouth at last.

Jenny named a romantic movie from the stack she'd brought with her. 'You don't rush back home, now,' she ordered. 'I'm nicely set up here for at least a week! Oh, and Bella said, if you rang, to remind you to take a photo of your new boss on your phone so she can see what he looks like!'

Well, that was a promise she was going to break, Cassie thought bleakly as she put her phone away. Nothing on this earth was going to make her risk her sharp-eyed daughter noting the similarities between her twin brother, Anthony, and Alessandro Marchese.

She even shivered at the prospect as she made herself go back up to the restaurant. The first thing she saw as she turned the bend in the stairs was Sandro standing by one of the tables across the room. Her gaze swept down the length of his back and his long, powerful legs trapped inside the elegant cut of his suit, then stayed lowered, her lips pressing together as she walked back to her own table and slipped into her seat as a burst of laughter erupted across the room.

'That guy knows how to make a good first impression,' she heard Ella say.

'Alessandro believes a relaxed and friendly working environment aides good will and increased productivity,' Gio Rozario responded loyally. 'You will like him, I promise you.'

I just bet, thought Cassie, unable to stop herself from watching Sandro move on to the next table and realising belatedly what he was doing. He was visiting each table in turn and she'd badly timed the moment she'd used the loo excuse because it was clear that he was moving around in this direction.

Now she was trapped, and knowing it heightened her tension to a point that she became acutely aware of his every move, every smooth syllable in his deeply modulated and beautifully accented voice. Each table he approached his designated spy came respectfully to his or her feet, then followed through by introducing each individual at the table complete with a pocket résumé, which fed Sandro fodder to weave into his disarming charm aimed to put everyone at ease with him.

Cassie was impressed by his tactics, though

she didn't want to be. She was annoyed with herself for the way her senses were sending tingling shock waves to every nerve-ending the closer to their table he came.

'Does he hire himself out?' Ella murmured curiously. 'I could do with someone like him around the next time I visit my family.'

Gio—they'd already been told to use his first name—laughed. 'Ask him,' he invited. 'Alessandro is pretty good with families, coming from a large one himself. Good at smooth set-downs too.'

He's pretty good with families…? Cassie felt a bubble of hysteria rise to her throat. For a horrible moment she thought it was going to break free. Then her slender spine stiffened as she picked up Sandro's presence arriving at the table directly behind her. She could even smell his subtly unique scent and feel the heat from his body, he was standing so close to the back of her chair.

Why Sandro? she asked herself tautly while everyone else was busy talking, joining in the light banter Gio Rozario and Ella were generating between the two of them. Why did *he* have to be the new owner of BarTec?

A flood of laughter suddenly erupted from the other table, encouraged to do so by a final comment made by the big man himself, then Cassie felt him turn to face them. Like a puppet pulled by his master's strings, Gio rose to his feet.

Snatching her hands down onto her lap, she balled them together in a tense-fingered clench as she listened to Gio begin the round of smoothly toned introductions and just prayed the screaming tension she was feeling was not showing in her posture or her face. He was standing so close to her one of his long, powerful thighs was in danger of brushing her naked shoulder so the skin there itched and tingled with tension and burned as it absorbed his body heat.

Gio's short potted history of each one of them was handed to his employer with a light touch which gave Sandro clues as to what to say to put each person at ease. He was fabulous at it, a true social connoisseur with that beautifully relaxed tone of voice and an accent that could probably turn the hardest female to melting mush. Half a dozen times Cassie tensed up inside when he reached out with an arm across her shoulder to shake the hand held out opposite her. Each time her awareness of him intensified to a place somewhere between a wildly hot resentment and sizzling self-defence.

Had he done it deliberately? Had he chosen to stand directly behind her chair so he could put off until the very last moment the point when he had to look her full in the face and acknowledge her?

'Ella Cole…' She picked up Gio's voice as if from a foggy distance. 'Ella is, she assures me, the lynchpin which keeps the accounts department running smoothly.'

'A secretarial tyrant in other words,' Ella happily described herself. 'Scary but nice,' she added as Cassie watched with the unblinking eyes of a bat as that long-fingered hand attached to a luxuriously dark silk-suited arm swept across her front to take Ella's hand.

It would be her turn next. She was the only one left. She was about to be forced into touching the hand that knew her body more intimately than any other man's hand, and she didn't know if she could bear it, didn't know if she could bring herself to touch him, be polite to him, pretend that all of this hurt and bitterness and anger crawling around inside her wasn't there.

'And Cassandra Janus.' Cassie tuned in to the sound of her own name being spoken, and felt a sickening tension grab her stomach as Sandro took a step to one side of her chair so that he could face her side-on.

This was it, she warned herself. Any second now he was going to offer her that hand and she was going to have to accept it—look up into his handsome, lying face and—

'Cassie is the bright new star in the accounts team...' Gio explained as the hand oh, so predictably appeared in front of her.

Cold now, so cold her fingers would not allow her to straighten them out of the tense clench she held them in, Cassie flicked her eyes up to his face. It was like being hit full on by six long years of agony. This close up he was even more shockingly spectacular to look at than she'd allowed herself to remember.

'Cassandra Janus...' he repeated slowly, turning *Janus* into the evocatively sexy *Janoos* the way he had used to do all those years ago, which dried Cassie's throat until she felt parched. And his eyes, those deep-set, heavy-lidded, rich dark brown eyes, were daring to look at her with such cool, polite interest as he added, 'I feel I should know the name from some-where… Have we met before by any chance?'

Had they met before…? Was he joking? Or was this his ruthless way of warning her to take care what she said? Dear God, Cassie thought as hysteria almost erupted from her in a shriek of high-pitched laughter.

Having to draw on every ounce of composure she had stored in her, 'No,' she managed as calmly as she could do, 'we haven't met before, Mr Marchese.'

Deliberately ignoring the way she'd all but bitten his name out, 'Alessandro, please,' he invited.

Cassie throbbed where she sat. He would have to nail her to a wall and threaten to throw knives at her before she'd call him by that name, she vowed fiercely. What did he want from her—blood?

And that hand still waited for her to place her own in it. Feeling light-headed with tension now, she managed somehow to uncurl her cold fingers and lift her hand to place it in his. An instant rush of electric recognition shot up her arm to gather like a hovering bullet just behind her ribs, close to her madly hammering heart.

As if he felt it too, his strong fingers closed over hers more tightly than they should.

'Angus headhunted Cassie from Jay Digital a year ago,' his spy continued with his pocket résumé with no clue as to what was passing between his boss and Cassie, 'which was probably the best move Angus ever made. I have been reliably informed that what Cassie does not know about financial performance and risk management could be written on the back of a postage stamp.'

'Interesting...' Sandro murmured, making Cassie cringe inside her own skin because he already knew she'd been studying for a MBA part-time when they'd met.

Yet she vaguely suspected that he'd barely heard a word that Gio was saying. His eyes still burned into her eyes, her hand still lay captive in his. And the electric tension they were generating between them just kept on building and building, dragging a frail, shaken breath from Cassie's lips. His ridiculously long eyelashes flickered as he lowered his gaze to her parted mouth and she shivered.

She watched a frown begin to crease his smooth features.

'Cassie is also one of those highly admirable people that successfully juggles the demands of her career with the demands of being mother to five-year-old twins,' Gio Rozario continued like a well-programmed robot.

Hearing the twins mentioned snapped Cassie back to reality. Unable to stop the bitter flash that spun out of her eyes into his, she snatched her hand back then dropped it onto her lap, where she returned it to a tense-fisted clench.

What happened next was pure drama. No one expected it. Certainly not Cassie, who was in the process of dragging her gaze away from his.

She heard a groan, felt Sandro grab the back of her chair with his hand and flicked a glance up to his face in time to catch the shaft of pain that creased it, followed by his swiftly draining pallor, just before she felt her chair start to shift.

After that she had no time to register anything

because her chair was being pulled right out from beneath her and somehow she was on her feet, trembling and shaking and staring as six feet four inches of powerfully built male dropped like a stone, taking her chair with him, to end up stretched out between two tables near her feet!

One of those dreadful pin-drop silences hung for a second. The whole thing was so out of the ordinary and bizarre, the entire room just froze in a breathless wait for him to curse or something then climb back to his feet.

But he didn't move, and in the next few skin-flaying seconds it took Cassie to register that he looked horribly lifeless, the rest of the room was erupting in a cacophony of sound that shattered the silence.

Gasps, cries, chairs screeching on the white marble flooring—she was vaguely aware of being pressed to one side as Gio rushed past her, followed closely by a flash of red. Shocked murmurs of, 'Did he slip?' 'Is he drunk?' 'Why isn't he moving?' ricocheted off Cassie's buzzing eardrums and she blinked, her shocked eyes swimming into focus on the crouching huddle that was Gio and the woman in red kneeling beside Sandro, urgently yanking at his tie and the collar of his shirt.

He looked grey—he looked dead.

Cassie heaved in a deep, thick, gasping breath of air and out of nowhere, just nowhere, she whispered, 'Sandro,' and was falling to her knees, all but knocking Gio sideways in her urgency to get to him.

'Sandro!' She cried out his name again, and sent a second shock wave rampaging around the stunned assembly.

CHAPTER THREE

'EXPLAIN to us what happened back there, Cassie.'

For such an outwardly genial character Gio Rozario had suddenly developed a core of steel. He was leaning against the edge of the desk in the restaurant owner's tiny back office, into which he'd hustled her, having been forced to bodily remove her from Sandro's prostrate form.

Standing beside Gio was the woman in the red dress who'd joined them a few seconds later. For such a beautiful creature, Pandora Batiste—as she'd introduced herself—had a way of turning her liquid brown eyes into glass, Cassie noticed as she gave a helpless shake of her head.

'I can't explain it,' she answered, still so badly shaken by what had happened that she couldn't keep her shivering limbs still where she sat.

'You dived on him,' Gio described.

Her mouth trembled, cold and shivery like the

rest of her because she still—still couldn't shrug off those horrifying seconds when she'd thought that Sandro had dropped down dead at her feet.

Because she'd wished for it—oh, so many times over the last six years when things had been tough for her—she'd wished with all of her aching heart to see Sandro dead at her feet.

'So did you,' she fed back, staring down at her right palm, which still pulsed with the reassuring beat of Sandro's heart from when she'd laid it against his chest.

'I know him, you do not,' Gio argued. 'Or we assumed you did not,' he then amended after a pause. 'He spoke to you…'

Cassie closed her eyes and saw the deep, dark chasms of Sandro's eyes when he'd opened them and looked into her face. 'Cassie—*Madre di Dio*…' he'd mouthed weakly, then he'd closed his eyes again and Gio had pulled her away from him.

'Please,' she said anxiously, 'will one of you go and find out how he is?'

'You called him Sandro,' Pandora Batiste took over, ignoring Cassie's plea. 'Nobody calls him Sandro. He despises it. He has been known to blow into a spectacular rage if he's ever referred to by that name. So why did you—a supposed stranger to him—feel free to use it?'

A wry kind of smile tilted Cassie's tense, pale lips. It was news to her that Sandro held such an aversion to the name, since it was he who'd given it to her in the first place. *Call me Sandro. Will you allow me to buy you lunch? A coffee, then? OK, may I just sit here and worship in silence…?*

'You know each other,' the glassy eyed beauty insisted. 'I witnessed your initial shock when you first caught sight of him in the bar. I felt Alessandro's shock when he saw you.'

With an effort Cassie lifted up her face to look at them both standing there, leaning against the desk with their arms folded and their eyes fixed on her while she sat shivering on her chair.

It annoyed her. Their whole superior and dominating attitude infuriated her. 'You have no right to interrogate me like this,' she protested.

'We are not interrogating you,' Gio denied the charge, 'we are simply concerned about what took place and—'

'Curious,' Cassie amended curtly, feeling a

return of some much-needed mental strength, 'but I will not have this conversation with you,' she informed the two of them. 'And I would be more impressed by your so-called concern for Sandro if you were out there with him instead of in here with me.'

'*Alessandro* is being taken care of—' It was Pandora Batiste who stressed the name.

'How can you know that?' Cassie looked at her. 'I would have thought your time could be better spent finding out *why* he passed out like he did!'

'That's what we're doing—'

'No, you're not. You're trying to bully information out of me that you have no right to demand. Is he drunk?' she asked sharply then. 'Has Sandro turned into a drunk, as well as a—?'

'As well as a what?' a different voice prompted from behind her.

Shooting to her feet, Cassie spun around to find the man himself standing in the office doorway. Her throat dried up. He looked dreadful, still as pale as death even if he was standing on his own two feet. And his eyes were too dark—as black as deep caverns hollowed into his skull.

'Are you all right?' She couldn't stop the strained question from leaving her aching throat.

He didn't answer. Flattening out his mouth, he just moved his eyes away from her to look at his two assistants and dismissed them with the barest shift of his dark head.

'Damage control,' he instructed as they both shot away from the desk in unison. 'Jet lag, migraine—I don't care what excuse you use so long as you make it convincing,' he added as they walked towards him, 'then find me a route out of here that does not require an audience.'

The door closed behind their retreating figures, leaving Cassie blinking at the mute obedience Sandro had commanded from them. If Pandora Batiste was his lover then she had to be a pretty darn subservient lover to take that kind of attitude on her beautiful chin.

As he returned his gaze to Cassie, she felt her own small chin shoot upwards in a defiant gesture brought on by what she had just witnessed. She was regretting now that she'd asked him how he was feeling, because he was clearly very all right, going by that tough performance. And if he was standing there like that and looking at her like that because he intended to bully her around in the same way, then he had another think coming.

Tension sparked in the atmosphere, generated mostly by her defiant stance. And still he said nothing, just slowly drifted his eyes over her as if he was carefully dissecting her inch by nerve-stripping inch.

How old was he now? she questioned as she suffered his scrutiny without allowing herself to flinch. Thirty-two—thirty-three? *If* he'd told her the truth about his age six years ago, that was. He'd given her a different name, so why not a different age? Anyway he looked years older right now as he stood there, leaning heavily against the door and with his face still drawn by the ravages of whatever it was that had sent him crashing to the ground in the first place.

Nor did he look so sensationally elegant, she noticed, her eyelashes flickering as she glanced down to where his shirt hung open at its snowy white collar and the knot of his tie rested low on his chest.

'You have not answered my question.'

Cassie lifted her cool gaze back to his. 'I

have absolutely nothing to say to you,' she informed him.

'You had plenty to say to my two assistants.'

'You think so?' Her arms snapped up to wrap around her narrow ribcage in a piece of body language that had to be screaming self-protection at him. 'Then why don't you go and ask them for your answers so you won't need to hold any kind of conversation with me?'

There was a short silence while his eyes narrowed. Her insides started to sting as if she were being attacked by a swarm of bees. 'You are very hostile,' he murmured eventually.

'Yes, aren't I?' Cassie agreed. 'And you don't think I should be?'

To her surprise he offered up a gut-stingingly attractive half-twist of a smile. 'To tell you the truth, I'm not sure.'

Baffled by that answer, Cassie pressed her lips together and waited to find out where he intended to go with this weird conversation. She had been expecting anger, she'd been expecting threats. He couldn't want the ugly truth about the real him to come out because it would tarnish his super-charming image. Closeting himself away in this room with her was, in her view, only helping to increase the fever of speculation that must already be rife out there.

'Look,' she said when she couldn't stand the silence between them any longer, 'neither of us wants this confrontation, Sandro. So why don't you move away from the door and I'll just leave?'

'Sandro,' he echoed and uttered an odd laugh, then he lifted his hand to rub at his forehead when it suddenly creased with pain again, triggering a twinge of concern inside Cassie she did not want to feel.

'I think you need to sit down,' she advised stiffly.

'Mmm,' he responded but made no move to leave the door.

Watching him rub at his brow for a few seconds longer, she let out a sigh and gave in to the growing pulse of concern that was nagging at her. Picking up the chair she had been sitting in earlier, she carried it across the room to set it down against the wall next to the door.

'Here,' she said abruptly. 'Sit down before you fall down again.'

When he swayed a little she was compelled to

reach out and grasp his arm. Firm, warm skin and solid muscle flexed against her palm and her fingers as he allowed her to guide him into the chair, folding his long body down onto it before leaning forward to rest his forearms on his knees.

'My apologies,' he said as Cassie snatched her hand away, his voice sounding thick and slurred.

Cassie said nothing, hating what was running through her now because it was all too complicatedly wrapped up in her son and the way Anthony could look when he was feeling poorly but trying his hardest to deny there was anything wrong with him until she gave him no choice but to accept it.

'I am not drunk,' this father of her children insisted from under cover of his massaging fingers.

So he'd heard her say that? 'Fine,' she responded. 'Whatever...' she added with a heck of a lot more indifference because she didn't like the way she was beginning to feel.

'I do not drink alcohol,' he persisted, probably driven to do so by her tone. 'If you had been observing me during the evening you might have noticed that I still had the same glass of wine I began the evening with...until it smashed to the ground when I did, of course,' he added with a dryness which seemed to give him back some energy, and he straightened in the chair.

He still looked like death. Cassie suppressed the need to shudder. 'Then you're sick,' she said, 'and if you're sick you need to see a doctor.'

'*Sí*,' he acknowledged. 'I will do so after we talk…'

That threat alone was enough to slam all her defences right back into place again. She tensed up, her body going rigid inside the little black dress. 'I don't think so,' she refused.

'You know me, yes?' he persisted. 'But for some reason you prefer to deny it.'

'What is this?' Cassie flashed out on a flare of anger. 'Some kind of weird game you're trying to play with me, or has your English deteriorated along with your ability to stand up on your own?'

He stood up, long, powerful legs thrusting up off the chair without a hint of a stagger, and, letting out a sharp gasp, Cassie was suddenly regretting the taunt when she found herself standing toe to toe with the lean, hard, very vital version of Sandro towering over her, as intimidating as hell.

'This is no game, I promise you,' he stated grimly. 'You speak to me as if I am your enemy. What is it you are trying to hide?'

'*I'm* trying to hide something?' Cassie's green eyes opened wide. 'Let's get this straight, Sandro. *You* blanked *me*! You turned your back on *me*! When you had no choice but to face me at the table you greeted me like I was some absolute stranger then still had the damn bare-faced cheek to *ask* me if we'd met before!'

'So you do know me!' Something bright burned out of the centre of his eyes and he stepped even closer, almost blocking out the light in the tiny back room.

Cassie started trembling, her senses clamouring like maniacs because he was too close now and they certainly knew him. They could feel him, smell him, even taste him. Six years without her so much as setting eyes on him meant absolutely nothing to them, she was discovering, especially when she had never let another man get this close to her since him!

'Back off,' she urged, turning her hands into ready clenched fists tucked tightly in against her ribs.

He didn't seem to hear her, and his colour was coming back, pouring rich olive tones into his skin, the power emanating from him now showing no hint of the weakness he had been displaying a minute before. 'You know me,' he repeated as if it was some kind of major breakthrough. 'What I need to know is *how* you know me!'

'I *don't* know you, Mr *Alessandro Marchese*,' Cassie flared up in hot opposition to his intimidating stance. 'Briefly, however, I used to know a real rat of a man called *Sandro Rossi*!'

There—it was out. He'd made her say it.

'Happy now?' Her green eyes blistered him a hostile glance. 'Though, why you needed me to admit to something we both clearly would prefer to forget is a complete mystery to me. Now *back off*,' she repeated icily, 'before I start yelling for help at the top of my voice!'

He went one step further and turned his back on her, reeling on the heels of his shoes. *'Dio mio,'* he breathed. 'Somehow I knew it.'

'Knew what?' Cassie all but shrilled at him.

'That we had met before.'

'And this,' she muttered, 'is the craziest conversation I've ever been involved in!'

'You don't understand…' As he spun around again, severe shock lashed his skin to the fabulous bone structure, making Cassie's stomach churn into trembling knots. 'You see, I don't remember you…'

Standing trapped by her own open-mouthed disbelief, 'How dare you say that?' she breathed.

He frowned. 'You are confused. I understand that.' Lifting a hand out towards her, when her green eyes sparked and her creamy shoulders racked backwards in violent protest, he sighed and dropped the hand again. 'This is the reason I said that we need to talk.'

Talk…? Pushing out a deeply scornful laugh, she said, 'When you can toss out lies as glibly as you do, Sandro, trust me, talking with you is a complete waste of time!'

'I do not tell lies!' he denied, stiffening up in furious objection to the charge.

'Then what about the one when you promised to come back for me then didn't bother?' Cassie challenged, firing up with hurt along with the question that had been burning holes in her heart for six long years. 'Or the one on the telephone when you denied we'd even met?—*"I don't know you. I don't want to know you. Please don't ring this number again!"*' she quoted word for crucifying, thick and hurtful word.

'I said that…?' He'd gone totally white again.

'Give me a break.' Dragging her eyes away from him because she did not want to see or accept that the way he kept changing colour like that had to mean he was being hit hard by something pretty shattering tonight. 'Once upon a long time ago I might have been an easy target where you were concerned—but not any more!'

'I do not believe I said something as cruel as that to you,' he breathed in thick denial, his long brown fingers clenching at his sides. 'It is not in my nature to speak to anyone like that!'

'Well, you said it to me.' Cassie had to tug her lips together when they tried to wobble uncontrollably because nothing had ever wounded her as much as those cruel words of rejection had done. 'Am I allowed to leave here now or have you got anything else you want to *talk* about?'

'No one has attempted to stop you from leaving,' he husked out.

Caught by the raw strain she'd heard in his

voice, Cassie made the stupid mistake of glancing at him again and saw that the hand was back up at his brow. Something creased up her insides to see such a big, powerful man standing there like that, but she refused to give the feeling room to grow.

'Thank you,' she said with icy curtness, and with a twist of her body she made herself turn to face the door.

Two seconds later she was on the other side of it with her eyes closed and her heart pounding as if she'd just run a mile. She had a feeling he'd swayed again but she had not hung around long enough to find out.

I don't remember you, her brain threw up at her in a seething flash of derision. If he didn't remember her then why had they had that confrontation at all?

The sudden sound of movement sent her eyes shooting open. The first thing she became aware of as her gaze became focused was that the whole restaurant seemed to have emptied while she'd been shut inside that tiny back room. The next thing to hit her was the low, buzzing sound of conversation floating up the stairwell and she realised that everyone must have moved back down to the bar.

Hovering at the top of the stairs, she swallowed tensely, trying to pull her ragged senses together before she had to go down there and face up to the full battery of BarTec curiosity she was certain would be waiting for her.

And she was trembling all over with reaction now. In the last couple of hours she felt as if she'd been fed through the emotional wringer a hundred times! First the shock of seeing Sandro standing in the restaurant bar entrance, then the stomach-curdling humiliation when he'd blanked her out.

I don't remember you...

He'd remembered her OK when he'd plied that heated scan down her body! And he'd remembered her when the delayed look of shock hit his face!

And—no, she couldn't go down there and face everyone. What was she supposed to say? Oh, we knew each other once. The memory of it drove him to drink wine until he was drop-down drunk.

I am not drunk...

Just another lie he'd fed to her. For what other

excuse was there when a strong, healthy man just collapsed like that?

'There is another exit,' his deep accented voice quietly murmured.

Cassie swung around on her slender heels, so startled her heart burst back into an overloaded beat. Sandro had come out of the office without her hearing him and was now in the process of closing the door. Her defences shot back up, her insides catching her with a tight, dizzying squeeze because he looked so different— again—as if he'd pulled up his own defences and now the cool, smooth corporate giant was back on show. He'd even done up his shirt collar and straightened his tie, she saw, her mouth going dry when her head decided to throw up an image of her teasing fingers doing that for him on the morning he'd left for Florence, all those years before.

'H-how do you know?' She had a fight to push the question beyond the fresh lump of hurt blocking her throat.

'I spoke to Gio.' He started walking towards her and as she tensed automatically Cassie thought she saw an angry glint move across his eyes but he strode right past her, though his voice fed out the same moderate coolness when he said, 'Follow me if you prefer to leave quietly. It's this way…'

Continuing to hover for a few more moments, Cassie wavered between her two choices that really were not choices at all. She either bit the bullet and ran the gauntlet waiting for her down there in the bar or she bit the bullet and let Sandro lead her out of here by a back door.

'Are you coming or not?'

He'd come to a stop in front of an emergency-exit door at the back of the room she had not noticed before. With a reluctance that had to show in her body language, she set her feet walking towards him, heavily aware she could not face those people downstairs. Although, she asked herself bleakly, how was she going to be able to face them in two days' time when she went into work on Monday morning?

With a touch from his long fingers Sandro pushed down the heavy bar to spring the lock on the door. Beyond it was a narrow set of stairs lit by emergency lighting that barely scraped the stair walls.

'Watch your step in those shoes; these treads are steep and narrow,' he instructed.

Lips pinned fiercely together, Cassie watched him go first, the width of his shoulders stretching almost wall to wall. Following him, she curled her fingers like talons around the sloping banister rail because they tingled so badly with a need to reach out and clutch at his shoulders for extra support on the rickety stairs.

At the bottom of the stairs was a tiny vestibule. As he reached it he turned and stretched out a hand towards her.

'Don't be squeamish,' he clipped out when she froze two steps up from him. 'My fingernails are not tipped with poison and the bottom step is loose and uneven. If this exit meets health and safety requirements I am in the wrong business,' he drawled as, once again, Cassie bit the bullet and settled her hand in his.

His strong, warm fingers closed over her cool, slender fingers. That same rush of electric recognition shot up her arm as it had done when she'd been forced to take his hand before. Concentrating all of her attention on the uneven steps, she arrived in the vestibule so close to him that her breasts brushed against his jacket lapel. Appalled by the pinch her nipples gave in response to the abrasive brush, with only the silk of her dress to act as a buffer, she very nearly did what she'd been trying not to do and fell off her spindly heels in her jerky effort to put space between them.

His other hand arrived low on her back to steady her. Instead of opening up a gap between them there was suddenly no gap at all. Unable as she was to stop it, a muffled breath left her throat and she looked up and was hit head-on by the glow of raw desire leaping out from his dark, dark eyes. His whole hard body pulsed with it. It was that instant, that hot, so stifling it held her breathless and horrified because the same dismaying heat was pooling low down inside herself, toying with intimate tissue that tugged and pulled.

Her throat hurt. She tried to swallow. The sense of being drenched in fine sexual static made her lips part to whisper something she couldn't even understand herself.

He understood it, though, because he muttered roughly, 'No wonder I'm struggling.'

About to demand what he meant, Cassie wasn't given the chance. Next second his dark head was lowering and she was receiving the full, burning impact of his passionate mouth on hers.

CHAPTER FOUR

HEAT poured into her bloodstream. He kissed her as if he'd been waiting to do it for years. He savoured it, explored the moist hollows of her mouth, guided her like some helpless puppet through the fiery pit of reacquaintance with the forgotten side of her own sensuality only this man had ever tapped.

His hand was restless on the small of her back, long fingers burning her through the fine layer of silk, stroking and kneading as they drew her further into the hardening bowl of his hips. The heat coming from him was heavy with the scent of his subtle aroma, the mobile seduction of his lips and the skilled intrusion of his tongue sinking her so deeply into a heady place of pleasurable memories Cassie found herself responding as a rolling mist of desire closed her in.

She felt small and weak and delicate as she

leant against him, could feel his heart pounding against the clenched fist she'd pressed to his chest when this had first begun. And she could feel her own heart racing against the tightening crush of her breast. Her legs had gone hollow again, that tingling sensation a wash of desire this time, attacking every nerve-end from her toes to her hips. When he breathed something against her mouth and moved against her the flash of sexual agitation she experienced flung herself back from him on a shocked, shaken gasp.

Eyes as black as ink bored into her for a second then flowed down over her heaving, slender, panting, trembling frame. His frown was back, the greying pallor, joined by a fierce, dark, pulsating frustration that scared Cassie even as her own shattered senses clamoured in direct response.

As he reached out towards her, 'No!' she cried out because she thought he was going to drag her back to him.

What he did was tighten the grim line of his mouth and gently hitch her dress up from its structured front. Her helpless whimper was of mortified agony when she realised why he'd done it. After that the silence between them sizzled. She'd never felt so helpless or so exposed or so *cheap* in her entire life. One kiss and she'd fallen to pieces. One kiss from a man she supposedly hated and she'd turned into—

'Oh,' she choked and shot into movement, spinning round and reaching out to grab hold of the heavy bar which held the exit door shut.

She was panicking—Cassie knew she was panicking and he was saying nothing. She could feel him standing there behind her like some—some—grim, silent reaper, probably disgusted with himself for kissing her at all!

Then his arms were coming round her; she felt the smooth, warm slide of his silk sleeves against her arms as with a gentle firmness he prised her fingers from the bar. Trapped like that, trembling and shivering at the same time, and acutely aware of every lean, hard inch of him, she watched through bright, burning eyes as he dealt with the heavy lock on the door.

Almost falling outside into the cool night air in an effort to put space between them, Cassie found herself in an alleyway that must run alongside the restaurant. It was quiet and dark, the shadowy bulks she could see across from her looking too much like lurking bodies to her fevered mind, though she knew they had to be rubbish bins. Still, she spun away from them to face what she thought—hoped—was the main street. She had to get away—she knew she had to get away before she did something really humiliating and fell into a fit of wildly sobbing tears.

Sandro. She'd just let Sandro kiss her stupid. How dared he—how could *she* have let him get away with it? She hated him, every single thing about him.

The door closed with a thud behind her and she jumped like a startled rabbit then went onto the balls of her feet. A strong hand clamped around her wrist to stop her running. The grimly silent way that he kept her still while he stepped close enough to strap his other arm across her back broke her control with a shrill, 'Let me go!'

'No,' he rasped. 'Look at the ground,' he instructed. 'This alley is cobbled. In those shoes you will not make it two steps without falling over or twisting an ankle or worse. And anyway, you are going nowhere, Cassandra Janus, until we've had our talk.'

Talk? He still wanted to *talk*?

'I h-hate you,' Cassie hissed out feverishly. 'That's talking.'

Keeping her clamped to his side, he set them moving and said nothing. She barely reached his shoulder and he was almost carrying her in his grim effort to keep her flimsy weight off her even flimsier shoes.

Electric storms came in different forms, she decided wildly as the electric storm Sandro was now generating sparked with a ferocious determination that held all the way to the lamp-lit main street and straight into the back of a waiting limousine conveniently parked at the kerb.

Shuffling inelegantly across the plush leather seat because he was not bothering to go around and climb in on the other side of the car, she felt his athletic bulk arrive beside her, folding down onto the seat, while Cassie was anxiously tugging her ruched skirt back into place over her exposed thighs. She dared a glance at him then wished she hadn't because he looked so stern, so grim and remote. It was only when he said something in curt Italian which set the car moving that her head twisted the other way and she realised they had a chauffeur to drive them. Even as she registered this unexpected mode of transport for a man who had used to drive himself everywhere in a racy soft-top, a black grated partition was sliding up in front of them and blocking the front compartment out.

Or them in.

'He—the driver—n-needs to know my address,' she pushed out in an attempt to snatch some control back here.

'If he were driving us there I would agree, but he's not.'

Stirred by his cool sarcasm, 'I suppose you think it's very macho to play the arrogant heavy!' Cassie flung out. 'But I can still see the fall-down drunk who embarrassed himself in front of his new workforce!'

His face swung around to slice a look at her. 'You never used to be this acid-tongued,' he hit back. 'Six years without me around to keep you in line has turned you into a harridan, *cara*!'

'I thought you didn't remember knowing me before,' Cassie returned sharply.

It shook him. She saw it happen. She watched his face drain of its wonderful colour and the pain come back to crease his brow. Shifting forward in the seat with an alarmed jerk, she went to bang on the partition because she thought he was going to pass out.

'Be calm,' he murmured, sensing rather than seeing what she was about to do because his eyes were shut. 'I have it controlled this time...'

This time *what*, though? Cassie wondered tensely as she remained perched on the edge of the seat, ready to call for help if she needed it, while Sandro continued to sit there with his dark head resting back against the leather seat and his long, powerful body looking worryingly sapped of strength.

And it was only then that she allowed it to truly sink in that something much more serious than too much wine was making Sandro behave like this. He looked really ill.

'Are y-you all right?' she asked when she couldn't stand his stillness any longer.

'*Sí...*' It was low and husky and it ran down through her like a hotline wired to her hips and thighs.

Cassie drew in some air, let it out again then, moistening her lips, which still felt hot and swollen after that terrible kiss, she gave in to the need nagging at her and reached out with a tentative hand and gently placed it on his knee.

'Sandro, please,' she begged huskily. 'You're frightening me.'

I'm frightening myself, Alessandro thought in an attempt to dry-humour himself out of this thick cloud which kept on blanketing him after each lightning strike. He managed to lift a limp hand and dropped it down on top of her hand as she would have withdrawn it from his knee. Small and fragile though her fingers felt to him, they seemed to possess a power of their own because he felt his energy begin to seep back through him.

'I suppose, Cassie Janus, you are wondering if this alcoholic requires a couple of shots of hard whisky to supplement his wine-soaked blood.'

'It isn't a joke,' she rebuked him sharply. 'And stop saying my name like that.'

'Like what?' Opening his eyes, he looked at her pale, strained, heart-shaped face with its beautiful emerald eyes darkened by concern for him.

'Like you're mocking me.'

Alessandro allowed a wry smile to stretch his lips. 'And here I sit believing I was mocking myself.'

'*And* you talk in riddles.' Sliding her hand out from beneath his and retreating into the seat, Cassie put as much distance as she could between them then sat staring out at London's night glitter, recognising famous landmarks which put them right in the centre of one of the city's most prosperous districts.

No cheap inner-city housing here, she thought dully. No dismal tenement blocks taken over by developers and crammed to their doors with as many apartments they could pack into them. Her own rented apartment shared the floor with two other tenants. She had two tiny bedrooms, a cramped living-dining room, a rabbit hutch for a kitchen, and the tiniest bathroom in the world. The hallway was not much bigger than the vestibule at the bottom of the restaurant steps back there where Sandro had—

Oh, don't go there, she groaned silently, shutting off her brain with a painfully tight swallow.

'You wear no wedding ring…'

'What?' Startled, she jumped, her head twisting round on her slender neck to find he was studying her hands.

'No rings,' he repeated.

'No. Why should there be?' she demanded defensively, her fingernails coiling into her palms.

'I did not say it as a criticism, merely as an observation.'

Her guarded gaze fluttered down to where his long-fingered hands lay relaxed on his lap. 'You wear no rings, either.'

'I am not the proud parent of twins.'

As if he'd reached across the gap between them and grabbed her by her throat, Cassie gave a choking gasp then froze. She'd forgotten the twins! How could she have done that? How could she have let herself forget that this man—this cold, heartless man—had rejected both her and her children before they'd even been born?

'I am presuming that you are not married,' he prompted in the same even tone.

He'd shifted his attention to her face now, carefully shielded eyes watching her expression in a way that made Cassie wish she knew what was going on inside his head.

'No,' she husked out.

'So who is taking care of them while you're out tonight—a live-in boyfriend perhaps?'

Her heart began to beat like a hammer drill. Where the heck was he intending to go with this line of questioning? 'No,' she said again.

'Then who?' he persisted.

'M-my neighbour.'

'So where is their father?'

Feeling as if he was reeling her in like a fish, 'Stop it, Sandro!' she hissed, her control just snapping.

'Stop what?' he questioned with skin-shaving innocence.

'Toying with me again!'

'I'm not toying with you,' he denied and even added a half-convincing frown.

'Then what are you doing? You know about the twins because I *told* you about the twins!'

He dared to look shocked. 'I don't recall—'

'What—*again*?' Cassie pealed out.

The car came to an elegant standstill. Twisting her gaze back to the window, she saw they'd stopped outside the entrance to a block of fancy apartments. The stark comparison to the apartments she'd just been thinking about clawed like a mockery down her spine.

Well, if he thought she was going in there with him he had another think coming, she determined. She'd taken more than enough of his madness tonight without having to deal with the pride-crushing effect of seeing how well he lived, while his children…

The chauffeur opened her door for her. Blinking up at him for a second, Cassie pushed out a stifled, 'Thank you,' then scrambled out of the car. The night air was chilly and she'd started shivering as she bent her head to open her tiny evening purse.

'What are you doing?' Sandro arrived beside her.

'I need my mobile to ring for a taxi—'

The hand that took the purse from her was smooth and slick. 'Not before we talk.'

As she stared up at him in gasping protest, he then took possession of her wrist with a grip like a velvet manacle and started trailing her towards the apartment-block entrance.

'But I don't want to go in there with you,' she told him furiously. 'I want my purse back and I want to go home!'

'Stop panicking,' he drawled. 'It's only ten o'clock. Your babysitter cannot be expecting you back yet.'

'That has nothing to do with it.' She tried a tug on her wrist. 'I have a right to decide for myself what I—'

His soft curse cut her off mid-sentence, sending her eyes shooting up to his face in alarm because she thought he was about to suffer another of those weird dizzy fits. But his expression was angry, not creased by pain. And when she followed the direction in which he was looking, Cassie saw through the plate-glass doors into the foyer a man standing leaning against the reception desk, chatting sedately to the security guard seated on the other side.

As the doors in front of them swung open like magic she saw recognition hit the stranger's face as he straightened up and smiled. He was young, smart and Italian if his dark good looks were anything to go by. Sandro bit out something in Italian which turned the other man's smile into a frown. A heated discussion struck up between them, which seemed to involve Sandro asking curt questions and the younger man replying with some firm questions of his own. The whole cut-and-thrust argument held Cassie fascinated and the porter engrossed. He seemed to understand them but Cassie didn't. When the stranger glanced at her and said something about her, Sandro exploded with a volley of words and a flick of his hand which she loosely translated as 'Keep your nose out of my business and get lost'.

Next Sandro was trailing her across the foyer and into the waiting lift. As the doors slid shut, Cassie had a final view of the other man's frowning impatience.

'Who is he?' she couldn't resist asking.

'My brother,' he answered.

Cassie looked at him. 'Why did you row with him?'

'Does it matter?' was the cool response that came back.

No, she supposed that it didn't. If Sandro liked to throw his weight around in that kind of manner with one of his family then it was none of her business, she told herself. And anyway, the lift doors were opening again and her attention returned to the way she was now being trailed out of the lift into the kind of inner foyer that screamed money at her from each luxurious corner, and revealed only one wide, glossy white door.

Using a card swipe, Sandro tapped a pin number into the wall-mounted keypad and the door swung free of its lock. On the other side of it was a large square entrance hall that her daughter would describe as 'really posh'.

With his long, arrogant stride he drew her across the hall's width and only dropped her wrist once they'd entered a beautiful living room with big and chunky brown leather chairs and sofas lit by soft golden lighting.

While Cassie was taking all of this in, he tossed her purse onto a side-table then was loosening his collar and tie again as he strode across the room. What she did not expect him to do was to throw himself down on one of the sofas. The moment he did it she noticed that the pallor was back along with the pain creasing his smooth brow.

'My apologies,' he murmured. 'I just need a few seconds to—shake this off.'

Silence clattered down while Cassie hovered, trying to decide what she should do next. Eyeing her discarded purse, then Sandro again, she knew exactly what she *should* be doing. She should be taking her chance while she had it, grabbing her purse and getting out of here. She didn't want this *talk* he kept on threatening her with. She didn't want to be here with him at all. He'd refused to let her *talk* six years ago when he'd rejected her panicked plea for him to listen to her. More important, he'd rejected the twins at the same time.

So why she was still hanging around here like a glutton waiting for more of the same punishment bothered her even as her feet took her across the floor until the front of her legs hit the arm of the sofa Sandro was stretched out upon. It was a huge thing, long and deep, but he easily measured its full length.

'Shake what off?' she asked him.

He didn't answer.

Feeling that unwanted stab of concern prick her defences. 'This is silly.' She sighed out. 'Sandro, you need to see a doctor….'

A half-smile twitched the corners of his mouth. 'A glass of water would be appreciated more.'

'Right…' Something to do. Cassie had already turned away when his voice came again.

'You will find some bottles in the fridge. The kitchen is—'

'I'll find it,' she interrupted him. 'I might be blonde but I'm not completely dumb. Hunting down a kitchen has got to be within my meagre mental capabilities even in this vast place.'

'Were you always this feisty?' he quizzed curiously.

'You mean you can't remember?' Cassie fired back. 'That's quite a selective memory process you've got going there, Sandro. You remember me but you *don't* remember me.'

'I remembered you while I was kissing you,' he returned huskily, 'and it was the sweetest thing I've tasted in years.'

Cassie stopped, her narrow shoulders wrenching backwards so her hair slithered like a silk curtain between her shoulder blades. 'Only an unprincipled rat would select that particular memory to mention,' she iced out.

Then she walked out, taking a teeth-clenching pleasure in pulling the door shut behind her with a slam she hoped doubled the pain in his head!

She came back to find him still stretched out on the sofa where she had left him but his jacket and tie were missing, which told her he'd attempted to get up, only to end up having to lie back down again.

Feeling that same stab of concern attack her insides as she walked across to where he lay, she stood trying to fight it for a good thirty seconds, then gave in with a sigh, and sat down next to him to reach out and place her fingers against his brow.

'You're cold,' she murmured worriedly.

'Never.' His mouth gave another one of those amused twitches. 'I am Italian. We don't do cold.'

'Be serious.' She frowned. 'Perhaps you have a virus or—'

'Mothering me, *cara*?' he taunted softly. 'If I remain lying here, looking pale and pathetic, will you soften your hostility towards me enough to listen to what I have to say?'

Cassie ignored the taunting tone. 'Why do *you* think you're feeling like this?'

Catching hold of her hand, Sandro lifted it away from his brow, long fingers enclosing her fingers, the dark, curling sweep of his eyelashes rising upwards to reveal the cavern-darkness of his eyes, now swept by fine golden flecks she'd only ever been able to see in them when she was this close. Those golden flecks gave the darkness life, added a glittering strength and shimmering vitality that was at odds with his pallor and his physically weakened state. And they held her captive, as they'd always been able to hold her captive. He was unfairly—too dangerously—attractive. He possessed the kind of dominating height and masculine body that probably turned most women weak at the knees. Yet, for all of his other assets, those eyes had been the pinpoint centre of Cassie's attraction for him from the first time she'd looked into them. And they still had the same power to draw her in, closing down her brain to a hazy, mesmerised state which made her feel totally exposed and hopelessly vulnerable to his magnetic pull.

'Because…' he said, the low, gentle husk of his voice barely registering in her stalled head, 'six years ago I was involved in a serious car accident which put me into a coma for three weeks and wiped my memory clean of something like six weeks of my life. Until tonight, that is, when I saw you standing across a crowded room and things started to come back to me in short, sharp, lightning flashes…and I want to kiss you again so badly I ache…'

Still gazing into those gold-flecked eyes, still trapped by their beauty and their mesmerising power over her, Cassie didn't move or speak. She didn't even breathe or blink. Then his words finally—finally sank in and on a strangled choke she wrenched her fingers free from his and launched to her feet.

The next thing she knew she was gasping for breath and staring down at her front, now dripping with ice-cold water which had splashed all over her because she had forgotten she was still holding the glass.

'Now look wh-what you've done,' Cassie shivered out. 'How—how dare you speak such a wicked pack of lies to me?' She refused to so much as acknowledge that last bit he'd said.

A soft mutter and Sandro was rising up from the sofa, the speed with which he went from pale and pathetic to energy-packed giant towering over her enough to spin her already dizzy head.

'Stop accusing me of lying,' he said, removing the now-empty glass from her nerveless fingers.

Cassie was trying to hold icy, wet, black silk away from her breasts without losing her dignity. She'd also soaked her face and the sides of her hair—water was dripping off the end of her nose and her chin. On a growl of impatience Sandro took possession of her wrist again, using it to haul her like a piece of quivering baggage back across the room and into the square hallway then across it into another room.

It was a huge white space of a bathroom with unforgiving lighting that set Cassie blinking as Sandro threw a switch. Grabbing a towel off the rail, he tossed it at her.

'Dry your front,' he instructed, then picked up a smaller towel and stepped up close to use it on her dripping face.

By now the water had warmed to her body heat and she was feeling calmer though no less shaken by what he'd said. 'What is it about you that makes you say these things?' she fired at him fiercely as she pressed the towel to her front.

'Think about it.' His fingers took possession of her chin to lift it upwards so he could dab the water from her cheeks. 'What's in it for me to make up a story as off-the-wall as this?'

He was right—what was there in it for him? 'You mean—you really don't remember me…at all?'

He drew the black arches of his eyebrows together. 'The way you put it a few minutes ago probably described it best—I remember you but I don't remember you.' The slanted half-smile he offered was as rueful as the answer itself. 'You are playing the starring role in some knock-out flashbacks, Cassie Janus. They hit me like a door that flings open in my head then slams shut again before I can get a proper glimpse at what is being shown to me. A couple of them have hit me like lightning bolts,' he grimaced, 'one of which stretched me out like a corpse at your feet.'

The mention of his corpse made Cassie shudder.

'You need to get out of that wet dress,' he said briskly, misreading the shudder for a shiver.

'No, I'm all right. Just a bit w-wet,' she dismissed impatiently.

He'd explained it all so casually but really there was nothing casual about it. He didn't remember her but he did remember her. The whole confusing evening began to make a mad kind of sense.

'H-how badly injured were you?' She was frowning again, already scanning him for signs of injury, as the idea of Sandro lying in a car wreck somewhere, hurt and unconscious, was so horrible to her that she couldn't stop herself from checking him out. The olive-toned skin stretched over his perfect bone structure with no signs of scarring or puckers or dints anywhere that she could detect. Dropping her gaze lower, she even checked out the unblemished skin at his throat then was scanning his arms and his chest as if she were equipped with X-ray vision and could see through his shirt. She did not notice how still he had gone, or that the long fingers holding up her chin had lifted away and now hovered a bare inch from her cheek, or that his eyes had narrowed.

Then she heard his low and very husky, 'If it helps you, *cara*, just say the word and I will take my clothes off so you can check me out more thoroughly….'

CHAPTER FIVE

CASSIE JUST FORGOT how to breathe.

He wasn't joking. He didn't even sound sardonic. A fire leapt into life deep down in her abdomen as belatedly she picked up the tension possessing his very still frame.

Sexual tension.

Looking up, she saw it burning out of the centre of his eyes like a flickering amber signal, felt its fierce heat prickle the surface of her skin, turning her own eyes a darker shade of green.

She wanted to say something cutting and dismissive—*needed* to say it—but the words wouldn't form in her head. He'd told her only a few minutes ago that he ached to kiss her again and she'd chosen to ignore the warning; now she felt like a rabbit trapped in the headlights of the car that was about to run her over. She parted her lips to utter a protest but made the mistake of running the tip of her tongue over the quivering, damp surface of her upper lip. As if he'd been standing there waiting for exactly that kind of sign from her, Sandro uttered a groan which seemed to scrape the very walls of his chest then moved his hovering fingers, spearing them into the silken fall of her hair to hold her head.

It was like a rabbit hit by a head-on collision. If he'd let go of her Cassie knew she would have folded down in a puddle of her own shattered emotions as he lowered his head and took driving possession of her mouth.

Nothing after that moment made a single ounce of sense to her as pure sensation took her over, springing life into every nerve-end to fling her like a fool to a place she'd believed she never wanted to visit again.

Why with him—why this man? she tried asking herself as her fingers released their grip on the towel so they could leap up to clutch at his shirtfront, her fingernails digging into warm, solid muscle as she gave herself up to his hot, deep, hungry kiss.

One single night spent in his arms six long years ago and her body remembered him with this strength and intensity. He felt so big and strong and so desperately familiar to her—as if she'd never been parted from him at all! Her heart was pounding madly, her head was spinning, her senses surging wildly out of control. It was *she* who gave in to the overwhelming force of it by abandoning herself to the hardening length of his long body and straining against him.

Sandro was trying to fight it. He should not be doing this, he tried telling himself. It was neither fair nor right. And he still felt really rough, though he had been trying to hide it. He felt as if his nice, tidy world was being ransacked by this beautiful creature called Cassie Janus, and he didn't need the added invasion of this ravaging race of sexual desire to cause him yet more havoc right now.

He even tried to draw back from it, tried to push her out to a safer distance. But this had been an evening of uncontrolled experiences, he admitted as her fingers stroked along the width of his shoulders then buried themselves in his nape so she could cling more tightly to him. With a throaty growl which did not sound very lover-like he closed his arms more firmly around her and lifted her right off her feet so he could delve deeper into the kiss.

He felt the hard tips of her breasts pierce his chest through his shirt and make an instant hot-wire connection with the burn taking place between his hips. Like that, he turned and carried her out of the bathroom. Like that, he found his way by sheer instinct into his bedroom and rolled them both down on the bed. He'd never experienced anything this powerful with any woman. He'd never wanted one as much as this. As she arched beneath his resting weight he shifted sideways and felt the urgent tremor in his fingers as he reached behind her to deal with the zip on her dress.

The structured bodice slithered down her writhing body, exposing the creamy white thrust of her breasts. Cooler air hit her heated skin and at last Cassie made a wild snatch for sanity, wrenching her pink, bruised, kiss-swollen mouth free so she could push out a trembling protest—

'Sandro, no, we can't do this!'

She didn't think he heard her. There was something almost bemused about the intense blackness in his eyes as he honed in on her exposed breasts. She squirmed beneath him as he folded his long fingers around one smooth, full mound then lowered his mouth to capture its taut, screamingly sensitive peak. Even as she cried out he was driving her so wild with pleasure she could only manage a grateful little whimper when eventually he reclaimed her mouth. Within seconds she was lost in it, drugged by her own uncontrollable desire for more of him—and more.

His shirt fell apart with the aid of her own urgent fingers, her hands feverish and greedy as they made contact with hair-roughened pectoral muscles moulding his powerful frame, and he shuddered, murmuring something hot into her mouth. The strength of her own hunger shocked her even as she sank into it like some sex-mad slave. She stopped trying to fight what she was feeling, she stopped trying to ignore the wild sensations he was creating as he stroked her skin. Desperate to touch him wherever she could do, she just couldn't keep still, slender limbs tense and restless as they moved against him. She was vaguely stunned to realise that all their clothes had disappeared. When he ran a seeking caress down the taut flatness of her stomach and stroked those long fingers into the hot, moist crevice between her thighs she just lost it altogether, gasping and trembling and urging him on with anxious strokes of her own restless fingers and helpless little words of need he answered in rich, dark Italian breathed like fire onto her receptive skin.

And she knew—still knew she should be stopping this, if only she had the strength of will. But she didn't have that strength and his sinfully pleasurable caresses were drawing her senses together in a twisting, squirming coil that forced her to whisper, 'Oh, God, Sandro, *please…*'

He arrived above her like a dark knight powered by a desire that slammed her hectic breath back down into her lungs. His eyes were burning flames of passion, the flesh covering his face tightly drawn. And his breathing was fast, his heartbeat uneven, the groan he uttered just before he recaptured her mouth more a warning that his control had fled. He drove into her with a single, long, deep stroke that dragged a quivering cry from her and a shuddering groan from him.

'Per Dio,' he groaned as her tender muscles

stretched then tightened in a sensual ripple along his full length.

Stars began exploding in her head as he started moving. Her fingernails latched on to the solid muscles in his arms as if she had to hold on for dear life. And she could feel each powerful inch of him inside her, his heat, his girth, even his pleasure as it transported each sensation he experienced with each new thrust and she was lost—abandoned to the wildly building fever of it. Her head was thrown back, her hair streaming down onto the pillow, her lips parted to let escape her soft, tense, helpless gasps. It was reckless, mindless, so beyond restraint that when her climax came it drew her taut as a bow beneath him, forcing a muttered oath from his lips when he had to support her slender frame in his arms so she could continue to take her pleasure and his thrusting weight.

Afterwards she lay in a daze of total mind-hazed shock. She didn't want to think, she didn't want to come down from where she still floated on a fluffy cloud of after-quivers because she knew that shame and soul-crushing dismay were waiting for her when she did finally drop back down to earth.

Sandro lay heavy on her with his arms still wrapped around her slender body and that feeling of being scraped out from the inside he'd felt earlier this evening, robbing him of the strength to move. They should not have done it and strange, swirling images were floating around his aching head. He'd never been so out of control before, did not know how it had happened or even why it had happened. It was as if someone else had been living inside his body, driving him on.

And those flashes were getting worse now, flinging open doors in his head and slamming them shut with a violence that set his teeth on edge. On an inner groan, he slid his arms from beneath her. *'Dio,'* he breathed on a thick, husky laugh aimed to lighten the charged atmosphere, 'did we ever get out of bed once we made it there?'

With Cassie still lying limp-limbed and trembling beneath him, his badly aimed joke brought her alive on a quivering flood of skin-flaying offence that had her pushing him off her before she reared up and swung on him wildly, landing the flat of her hand hard against the side of his face.

Gasping and shaking and dimly horrified by her own outburst of physical violence, 'Are you referring to the single night we spent there before you upped and left me?' she sliced into him chokingly. 'You really like to live up to the wham-bam-thank-you-ma'am, macho-rat remit, don't you, Sandro? Two weeks wooing me and one night screwing me. Mission accomplished, so *forget* that one, leave her pregnant and move on to the next!'

Having collapsed on his back beside her, Sandro took the full blast of her shaking anger the same way he'd taken her slap to his face—with total stillness, nothing showing on his face now except her finger marks standing out on his cheek. And his lack of reaction only made Cassie want to hit him again; she wanted to pummel his chest with her fists!

Instead she scrambled off the bed with a snaking move of trembling limbs and looked wildly around for something with which to cover herself up. She saw Sandro's shirt lying draped half on and half off the side of the bed and shuddered, spinning away from it. She would rather be flayed alive than wear that next to her now-cringing flesh. How dared he make a joke of what they'd just done here? How had it happened? How had she let him reduce her to this? Grabbing a pillow up off the bed, she hugged it to her front, a well of hot tears building in her throat. Oh, God, she hated herself—she hated him! And her legs could barely hold her upright, her insides still singing like sinful traitors triumphing over what Sandro had done for them.

On a stinging shot of shamed energy she began urgently gathering up her clothes, refusing to look at him, refusing to notice how he was still lying there, saying nothing, or how the hand was back up at his face, long fingertips pressing into his creased brow.

Clutching the pillow to her front along with her skimpy jumble of clothes now, she turned and headed for the door. She had to get away. She just had to—

'I cannot believe I did that to you.'

The husky sound of his denial froze Cassie taut and quivering in the doorway. 'Can't or don't want to believe it?' she shook back.

Without thinking, she spun to look at him in time to watch him roll off the bed to land beside it on his feet. Each beautifully toned inch of him was captured by the light from the single lamp burning golden by the bed, sweat-glossed sleek, powerful muscles that expanded and contracted in a lithe display of masculine potency that turned her ravished muscles to hateful, trembling mush.

Why did *he* have to be the only man who could do this to her? 'If you ask me, Sandro, your biggest problem is that you don't seem to want to know yourself—which in my view makes a complete mockery of your so-called lost memory!'

He flinched, one of his hands sweeping out in a sharp, slicing gesture meant to cut her bitter words to shreds. Shaken by the violence of the action, Cassie just stared as he jerked into movement, striding across the room to disappear through a door, closing it behind him with a quiet thud that left her standing there with her heart writhing around in her chest in self-disgust at what she'd let him do to her—again.

A sob of revulsion broke free from her throat and she dropped the pillow and spun around to leave the bedroom at a wild run, making for the bright white bathroom where her foolish downfall had begun. The harsh lights hurt her burning eyes as she dragged on her flimsy briefs and fumbled feverishly with the zip on her dress. She hadn't found her stockings but she didn't care, she told herself as she wriggled her bare toes into her shoes.

All she wanted to do was to just get the heck out of here without having to face him. As she turned towards the door she caught a glimpse of herself in the mirror and a stinging flood of tears lashed her aching throat. She looked like a plump-lipped, hot-cheeked lush! Her hair was all over the place, its waterfall layers all tangled and mussed, and her eyes were so dark she looked as if she'd been indulging in some kind of drug!

Which she had in a way, she thought helplessly as she wrenched her gaze away from her gut-crawling image. She'd indulged in the drug of irresponsible sex, and coming down from it was the worst feeling she'd ever experienced! Snatching the bathroom door open, she sped across the hallway and into the living room with the intention of retrieving her purse from where Sandro had tossed it and getting the heck out of here!

Only to find herself jerking to a sinking, shuddering standstill when she saw Sandro there in the room.

He was standing beside a cabinet which stood open to reveal a selection of bottles and glasses. He'd pulled his trousers and his shirt back on but half the buttons were left unfastened and his feet were bare, the smooth style of his hair roughed up. He looked pale with strain but hard and grim and he held a glass slotted in his fingers that definitely did not have water in it.

'Whisky,' he said, catching the fluttering direction her gaze had taken. 'I decided I might be better off becoming a drunk before you lay any more shocks on me.'

'There are no more shocks.' Cassie struggled to get even those few words past the thick blockage in her throat.

'You think not?' He scraped a set of fingers through his hair, oddly managing to smooth it without, Cassie was sure, that being his intention. 'Try climbing inside my head, *cara*,' he invited grimly. 'It is a minefield of shocks and questions.'

He took a gulp at his drink.

It was yet another change in his personality Cassie found she had to struggle with. She'd seen the ultra-sophisticated businessman and the smooth expert charmer. She'd seen shock completely debilitate him and felt the explosive thrust of his anger scare her almost out of her wits. He'd been weak, he'd been strong, he'd been frighteningly vulnerable and ruthlessly passionate when he'd taken her to his bed. Right now he just looked unbearably cynical and chillingly remote, as if he'd slammed *his* defences into place.

And maybe that wasn't a bad thing, she decided as she hovered tensely on the threshold of the room, desperately wanting to snatch up her purse and just go, yet held glued to the spot by a bubbling growth of concern because she could see the strain of what was happening to him was really making itself felt now and he looked so dreadfully pale.

'Sandro, please, don't drink that,' she murmured unsteadily. 'I don't think—'

'Tell me the date you claim we were together,' he cut in right over her.

'We *were* together!' Cassie instantly flared up.

'All right,' with another one of those angry slashes with his hand, 'tell me *when* we were together, then!'

Needing to take in a breath of shaky air, Cassie named the date.

Sandro made a jerky movement that was almost a flinch. 'For how long?'

'I've told you this too—'

'Then repeat it. How long?' he bit out rawly.

Pressing her lips together, she had to push herself beyond the shame barrier before she could answer, 'Two w-weeks.'

'Two weeks,' he echoed in a thick, cursing voice. Then he really scared her by dropping like lead into the nearest chair and made that gesture with his fingers, pushing them up against his brow. 'Are you claiming that we managed to conceive twins in only two weeks?'

'N-no.' Having to bite back the desire to object to the way he had put that, Cassie gave in to her own trembling legs and walked over to a chair to sit down. 'It took you two weeks to get me to go to bed with you and only one n-night to conceive the twins. The next morning you said you had to fly back to Florence. You promised you would be gone for only a few days but you never came back.'

'I couldn't come back.' Lowering his hand from his brow, he continued the story from his point of view. 'The accident happened and I lost six seemingly vital weeks of my life.'

'Will you *stop* this, Sandro?' A sudden flush of hot anger launched Cassie back to her feet. 'Your lost weeks have nothing to do with this!'

His head shot up. 'How the hell do you come to that crazy conclusion?'

'But I *told* you this too,' she cried out. 'I called you on your mobile. You barely gave me the opportunity to speak before you hit me with, *"I don't know you. I don't want to know you. Please don't ring this number again..."'*
As he jerked to his feet Cassie shuddered because those harsh words were etched in fire on her brain. 'It was quite a brush-off,' she continued with a thin laugh that didn't even touch base with humour. 'If I had been in a better frame of mind I m-might have appreciated just how callous you could be. But at the time I was more concerned about myself and the—the twins I'd just found out I was

carrying. When I tried to tell you about them you put the phone down on me!'

'But I do not remember this telephone call!' he thrust out angrily.

Eyes like green fire leapt into contact with his eyes. 'That conversation took place eight weeks after you left me, Sandro. Are you now saying that your memory loss scans *eight* weeks instead of six?'

In the thickening silence that gathered after that piece of blazing sarcasm, Cassie wondered why she was bothering to repeat any of this when once again he gave no reaction, not even a wince.

'Even if you did not remember m-me,' she went on unevenly, 'a less callous man would have hesitated long enough to ask himself if there was a chance I could belong to his lost weeks.' And she'd been so scared, almost weeping, begging him to listen to her. 'But you weren't interested enough to want to bother to do even that, were you?'

Still he said nothing. And he was emulating a slab of rock now—because he could no longer defend himself against what she'd said?

Probably, Cassie decided as the feelings of bitterness flooded back into play and she turned to walk over to the side-table and picked up her purse. 'Just do me a favour, and stay right away from me,' she husked out shakily. 'If you decide you want contact with my children then you will have to go through my solicitor because I don't want you anywhere near them.'

And this time she was leaving, Cassie told herself. This time she was *not* going to look back.

As she walked to the door the sound of something falling shattered that vow almost as soon as she'd fixed it inside her head. She swung around, her blood already running cold because she knew what she was going to see even before her eyes locked on to Sandro lying stretched out on the living-room floor.

Like an action reply of the last time he'd done this, she was on her knees beside him before she'd realised she'd moved.

'Sandro...' she breathed, reaching out to touch her trembling fingers to his cheek. His skin felt horribly cold and clammy and the grey cast to his face sent alarm bells jangling up through her insides.

Getting to her feet again, she raced out of the room and down the hall to the kitchen. A minute later she was back on her knees beside him again with a damp cloth and a glass of water that was pretty useless, she thought wildly when he was still showing no sign of coming round.

'Come on, Sandro…' she urged tensely, pressing the dampened cloth to his brow then his mouth then his brow again—touching him because she needed to touch him but without a single clue as to what she should be doing to help him.

Another minute went by and he still wasn't moving. And like a safety switch built inside her, the more practical side of her nature swung into play. He needed a doctor—maybe even an ambulance. Glancing around for her purse, she saw it lying halfway across the room where she must have dropped it as she'd run. She was about to scramble up and get it, when another phone started ringing and her eyes spun dizzily to look at Sandro's suit jacket still lying across the back of a chair where he'd draped it.

Without thinking about it she stretched out to

drag the jacket towards her then reached into the pocket and pulled out the phone.

'Alessandro, it's Gio. I've just had a call from—'

'Oh, thank God,' Cassie breathed with shaking relief. 'Gio, it's Cassie. Sandro has collapsed again. He needs a doctor or an—'

'Leave it to me.' To his credit, Gio didn't waste time demanding explanations, he just said, 'I'll have someone there in a few minutes.'

The next five minutes dragged by in a frightened haze while Cassie sat beside Sandro, hugging her knees to her chin with one tense arm while the other hand rested against his chest so she could feel the comforting beat of his heart. He still hadn't come around by the time the door bell rang, forcing her back to her feet to go and answer it.

Gio stood on the doorstep along with the man she'd seen in the foyer when they'd first arrived here this evening.

Gio said, 'This is Marco, Alessandro's—'

'Brother. Yes, I know.' Cassie glanced at the other man with a strained smile quivering on her lips, which he did not return.

'Where is he?' he demanded brusquely.

A bit shaken by his attitude, 'In—in the living room,' she responded, and he brushed past her into the apartment.

'Marco is also a physician,' Gio explained dryly as he too stepped past her.

And the brother's brusque manner began to make sense. The argument between the two brothers down in the foyer must have been about Sandro's blackout at the restaurant. Someone must have called Marco to meet his brother here but Sandro had sent him away.

Following the two men into the living room, Cassie lowered herself into a chair to watch helplessly as both men went down on their knees beside Sandro. Her heart was pumping very slowly now and she had a vague suspicion that she might be going into shock because she couldn't seem to feel anything else at all.

Even when Sandro showed signs of coming round she still didn't feel anything. Eventually he sat up, holding his head in his hands. His brother was murmuring something to him and Sandro was answering in low, thick Italian. All three men seemed to understand what had happened, which left only Cassie without a clue.

A severe shock could make a woman faint, she knew that. It could make a man black out. But she knew that what she had witnessed with Sandro was much more than that.

Then she heard Marco murmur in English, 'We need to get you to bed, Alessandro.'

And she came alive like a phoenix rising up from the ashes of numbed senses. Without saying a word she just leapt up and ran out of the living room and into Sandro's bedroom, then began rushing around it, madly trying to tidy the evidence of their recent activities in there before the others came in and saw it and guessed what had been going on.

She found her stockings and Sandro's socks then remembered with a sharp jolt that he wasn't wearing any shoes. Gio and his brother had to be curious as to why he wasn't, which meant...

Oh, shut up! she slammed at the riddling squirm of her own guilty conscience and was just straightening the rumpled blue coverlet when a sound by the door made her look up then go perfectly still.

Sandro was leaning heavily against the door-frame. 'I see we are both on the same wavelength, which makes a change…' he drawled, glancing around the hastily tidied bedroom.

'You look dreadful,' Cassie breathed, slowly straightening up.

'I feel it.' He grimaced. 'I'm sorry. Did I scare you again?'

Her throat felt so thick she couldn't get any words out, so she swallowed tensely and nodded. Then because he looked as if he was going to keel over again she went and slid her arm around his waist.

'Y-you need to be in bed.'

One of his arms arrived heavy across her shoulders. 'So I do,' he agreed.

'Let me call your brother and Gio to come and help you—'

'You can't. I sent them packing.'

'But—why?' Cassie gasped out.

'Their presence here embarrassed you.'

'What has that got to do with anything?' She flashed a sharp green look at him. 'Your health is more important than my embarrassment. Not five minutes ago you were lying unconscious— again!'

'Now I'm not,' he responded with cool logic,

'though I cannot guarantee to remain upright for much longer, so if you think you could…'

'Oh.' Cassie tightened her grip on his waist. 'Let's get you to bed, then.'

'Best invitation I've had all day—'

'Don't you dare make a joke of it!' she choked out. 'Have you any idea what it's like to watch you drop like that? I thought you were dead! I thought you'd suffered a m-massive heart attack or s-something and I…'

'OK—OK,' Sandro cut in soothingly. 'Don't start weeping on me, brave Cassie. Just help me across the room so I can fall on that bed.'

Pinning her trembling lips together, she did as he bade her. Brave Cassie indeed. She hadn't felt brave while she'd sat beside him. She'd felt helpless and useless and scared.

As they reached the bed Sandro swung his arm off her shoulders and sat down heavily, then just keeled over like a drunk.

Still without allowing herself to say another word, Cassie busied herself doing the mothering thing and placed a knee on the bed so she could reach across to the other side of him and catch up the cover so she could flip it over his length.

'I'm not cold,' he told her, his ink-dark eyes fixed on her pale profile.

'You feel it,' she insisted.

'I thought you did not want to come near me again.'

It was a taunt, a soft and husky-voiced kind of taunt that made the muscles around Cassie's heart flutter in response. She opened her mouth to insist that she didn't want to be near him, then on a heavy sigh she changed her mind and sank down beside him on the bed, slumping her shoulders in a weary gesture of defeat.

'Tell me what's wrong with you,' she requested.

He was silent for so long that she thought he must have gone to sleep but when she turned her head to look at him he was still watching her through those unfairly captivating, fathom-dark eyes and a lump formed in her throat because— oh, dear God—she knew deep down inside her that she was still in love with him.

'They knew what was going on—Gio and your brother the doctor,' she prompted. 'I saw it in their faces the moment I opened the door to them. For ninety-nine per cent of the time you're so strong and vital I would challenge a tank to try and knock you over…' without knowing she was doing it, she reached out to rest her hand against his chest above his beating heart '…but I've seen you drop twice now, and you usually rub your brow and frown just before it happens as if—as if—'

'I'm in pain, which I am,' Sandro finished for her. 'The car accident left a—pressure on my brain which makes itself felt now and then.'

'So it isn't just m-me that causes it?'

She sounded so vulnerable when she said that, Sandro released a small sigh and his hand arrived to cover hers. 'It can be bad sometimes…' He hedged the question.

'Bad enough to make you pass out—a lot?'

'No,' he denied. 'Occasionally—rarely. I get these flashes of memory which hit me out of nowhere. They're sometimes followed by…'

'A complete shut-down.'

'*Sí.*'

'Can anything be done to ease the—pressure?'

'Can we talk about the twins instead?'

The twins…! Once again, Cassie was hit by a jolt of reality. 'Oh, heck,' she gasped, jumping to her feet. She'd done it again and forgotten all about the twins! Flicking a glance at her watch, 'It's late. I've got to go…'

'To relieve the babysitter?' He sounded grim again.

'Yes.' Looking around her, trying to remember where she'd stashed her stockings in her rush to hide the evidence of what they'd been doing in here, she explained, 'Jenny is very good but I promised her I would be back home by midnight—'

'Like Cinderella.'

'No…' impatience added bite to her answer '…like a single mother who cherishes a reliable babysitter so does not take advantage of her time!'

Sandro frowned at his watch then, noted what Cassie already knew—that she had only fifteen minutes left to her midnight deadline—and with a lithe stretching movement he discarded the cover and rose up off the bed.

'I will take you—'

'No!' Cassie cried out. 'You should have stayed where you were! I can call a cab—'

He turned on her, scowling now as if she'd offended his masculinity. 'Either I take you home or you will use my driver!' he slammed out with a force that made Cassie blanch.

'All right!' she shot back in quivering reaction. 'I'll let your driver take me! I don't know why you needed to shout.'

'*Grazie,*' he teethed out, and reached over to pick up a phone by the bed.

Cassie bit into her bottom lip to stop herself from saying anything else. Having stabbed in the required number, he pushed the phone to his ear and showed her the length of his back.

To Cassie it was another one of his cold dismissals. In response to it she spun on her heel and walked out of the bedroom. Every time they held a conversation, they went from calm into a raging storm without any pause in the middle. Now her insides were fizzing with—she no longer recognised what it was that was going on inside her or what was making her wait around in the hallway until he joined her there.

When he appeared, striding towards her with his expression still drawn and now irritable too, she could not stop herself from asking, 'Will you be all right here on your own?'

'Don't make me out to be so pathetic,' he bit

out. 'And stop looking at me through those anxious emerald eyes because it turns me on like a flaming gas jet! Just do something sensible and go, Cassie.'

He pulled the door open then just stood there, expecting her to get out—wanting her to get out even though he claimed she turned him on.

Well, there was no sign in him of gas jets right now, she recognised, just a hard, grim, remote man.

So she left, her lips pressed together to stop them from quivering, and her eyelashes trembling against her cheeks. He stood at the door and watched her until the lift doors closed between them. Then, like a fool, she parted her lips and let them quiver, let her eyes open wide and fill with wretched, unwanted, weak tears.

CHAPTER SIX

CASSIE let herself into her tiny apartment virtually on the stroke of midnight. Everything was quiet and soothingly normal, only the muted sound of the television seeping out from the living room to tell her that anyone else was here.

Taking in a deep breath, she opened the door to find Jenny sitting in the armchair watching TV just as she'd imagined her, with her feet up on the coffee table and the almost empty box of chocolates lying on her lap.

'Oh, hello.' Jenny smiled at her, straightening her round, comfortable shape up in the chair. 'You've timed it nicely because my film has just finished. Did you have a nice time?'

I wish, Cassie thought heavily. 'Yes,' she heard herself answer with a calm that didn't sound as unnatural as she feared it would. 'Have the twins behaved themselves?'

'Perfect angels. Not a single peep out of them.' The older woman came to her feet and plied her with interested questions about her evening while she gathered together her bits and pieces and hunted down her discarded shoes.

'W-would you like a cup of tea before you go?' Cassie found her good manners from somewhere.

'No, thank you, love. I'd just had one before you arrived home.'

A few minutes later and Cassie was closing the front door on Jenny's disappearing figure then turning to lean back against it with a sigh. She'd never felt so battered and wrung out in her entire life.

Then she was pulling herself together and peeling herself away from the door to go and check on the twins. She found two peacefully sleeping faces highlighted by the tiny night lamp set on the table between their beds. Anthony was lying sprawled on his back with his duvet half kicked off him, his thick, dark hair ruffled in a way that made Cassie's heart squeeze because it looked so like Sandro's had looked before his fingers had unwittingly smoothed his hair back into place. Bella lay curled neatly on her side as she usually slept, her pale blonde hair streaming out behind her in a silken gold swathe.

They both looked so young, so sweet but so very vulnerable. How were they going to feel about a father they hardly knew anything about if Sandro decided he wanted a role in their lives?

It didn't bear thinking about. Cassie was too *scared* to think about it. And, selfishly, her fears were mostly for herself. The twins had always been just hers to love and to be loved by. There hadn't been a single second since their birth that she hadn't loved and cherished them with all of her heart. In everything she'd done since she'd known she was pregnant and alone, she'd always placed their well-being first—in her choice of employment, in her choice of nursery accommodation, paying over the odds to secure the best care available for them and negotiating a flexible timetable with her employers so she could work the best hours to suit the twins' needs. When Angus offered her this chance to come up to London to work for him, it had been the much larger wage packet and his kind offer to let her rent this flat from his property portfolio on reduced terms that had clinched the deal for her.

Still, it had been tough sometimes to reach the end of the financial month still solvent but she'd done it. Cassie was proud of that achievement—fiercely proud. However, she would be willing to bet that Sandro wouldn't view their tiny flat and their threadbare second-hand furniture as anything to be proud of.

Closing the twins' bedroom door as quietly as she had opened it, she stepped into her bedroom next to theirs. Both bedrooms were short on space but the twins had the larger room simply because it was practical while the two of them shared.

What happened, though, when it was no longer practical for them to share? she wondered suddenly. What happened if, now he'd sold BarTec, Angus decided it was time to sell his property portfolio too and she found her reduced rent bumped up to the same as that of the other tenants, as it was bound to be?

She thought of Angus again on a sudden wave of guilt because she was thinking selfishly once more instead of feeling concern for her father's old friend and his failing health. She made herself a promise to visit him next weekend—it couldn't be this weekend because the twins had a birthday party to attend. Angus loved it when she took the twins on a visit. He might be a die-hard bachelor and seriously ill but he maintained that an afternoon spent with her and the children was a better pick-me-up than any doctor could prescribe for him.

And her dress needed dry-cleaning, she saw as she slipped it onto a hanger. The water spill had dried and left the embossed silk looking like crushed tissue paper. Teach her not to indulge in an expensive dress with a dry-clean-only label, she told herself—and knew she was thinking about mundane things to stop her head from thinking about what she'd just done with Sandro.

She almost jumped out of her skin when the phone beside her bed started to ring. Diving at it to pick it up before the shrill ring disturbed the twins, she flicked out a sharp, 'Yes?'

'All right...' the sound of Ella's voice hitting her eardrums had her sinking wearily down on the bed '...start talking. What's the history between you and our sexy new boss?'

'There isn't any history,' she lied, wishing with every aching pulse she had in her that it was the truth.

'Pull the other one, Cassie. That guy almost ate you up and you almost spat him out in disgust. And all of that came *before* you laid him out cold on the floor!'

'I did not lay him out,' she denied.

'No, you just jumped on him afterwards, called him *Sandro* and almost wept all over his shirt. The next thing we know you're being hustled away into a back room and we're being spun a line about jet lag and migraine headaches and get a glimpse of neither one of you again. You know the guy, Cassie,' Ella insisted. 'Everyone at BarTec knows you know the guy. Even the MD confirmed that our new boss couldn't keep his eyes off you all evening. And the beautiful Miss Batiste was not happy about it if the way her lovely dark eyes had turned cat-like was a judge.'

'She can keep him. I don't want him,' Cassie burst out unthinkingly then could have bitten off her unruly tongue.

'Oh, wow,' drawled Ella, 'that sounded to me like a bitter woman talking.'

'Look,' she said, straightening her wilting shoulders and hunting around for an explanation that would shut Ella's curiosity up, 'I don't *know* him exactly but I—I used to know an…acquaintance of his…' which wasn't an outright lie, she reflected grimly '…and that's it. No mystery.'

There followed a long silence that made Cassie's tense fingers pluck at the quilt covering her bed. Then Ella spoke again. 'He knows the twins' father.'

Cassie closed her eyes on a silent groan. 'Will you *please* put your imagination to bed?' she pleaded. 'And while you're at it put yourself to bed at the same time, because that's where I'm going!'

'Yeah, right,' mocked Ella. 'To dream of no-good Italian love-rats that get a girl pregnant then dump her, and their handsome *acquaintances* that drop down dead in shock when the twins are mentioned.'

'Weird dreams for you to have, sweetie,' Cassie mocked right back. 'I wonder what the bodybuilder would think if he knew…?'

'Clever,' Ella acknowledged. 'Now tell me where you disappeared to with him.'

As she discovered she was staring at the black dress on its hanger, Cassie's next excuse lit like a lightbulb in her head. 'I managed to drench my dress in the—commotion,' she said, telling yet another lie that wasn't quite a lie. 'His driver brought me home.'

And right there on the back of that second twist on the truth, she realised she'd found a couple of reasonable excuses which would allow her to show her face at work on Monday morning. Sandro was a distant acquaintance. He'd sent her home in his car.

'Listen, Ella,' Cassie murmured seriously, 'I want you to keep your suspicions to yourself about my connection to Mr M-Marchese—' she *hated* saying that name '—being more than a distant acquaintance to me. I can't afford to put my position at BarTec at risk because rumours go rife that make it too uncomfortable for us to work together there.'

'Calm down,' sighed Ella, 'I'm your friend, not your enemy. You should know I wouldn't dream of saying any of this to anyone else but you!'

'Thanks,' Cassie mumbled. 'Sorry,' she added.

'So I should think. You know,' her friend added slowly, 'Jason Farrow also shot his big mouth off about your father and Alessandro Marchese's father both being friends with Angus.'

'Really?' Cassie was so surprised by that piece of information she couldn't stop letting Ella know it.

'If you need a good excuse to let loose on BarTec's curious minions, I would use that connection if I were you. Especially since the MD has already started that ball rolling for you.'

'Bless you, Ella,' Cassie whispered, feeling stupidly weepy now.

'Don't mention it,' Ella replied. 'Maybe one day you'll trust me enough to give me the real story, hmm?'

Maybe, Cassie thought, knowing that Ella already had a pretty good handle on it anyway.

The weekend passed by on a whirl of busy normality with no sight or sound of Sandro—if she didn't count the number of times he visited her dreams, waking her up with the hot drive of his body joined intimately with hers. Dreams like that were so very shocking she'd huddled beneath her duvet, horrified by the vividness of her imagination and ashamed by it. She hated him, she tried telling herself. She didn't understand what had made her do what she'd done with him. It whittled away at the self-belief she'd spent all these years earning back since the last time he'd done his best to wreck it.

The shy and introverted twenty-two-year-old working hard to prove her junior position at Jay Digital, as well as recover from her father's recent illness and death, just hadn't acquired the necessary weapons needed to deal with someone as handsome and charming and sexy as Sandro Rossi when he strode into her life. He'd *wooed* her like some old-fashioned suitor. He'd been so intense when he told her he'd fallen in love with her. He'd vowed to make her happy for the rest of her life. He'd said and done all the right things in the right order to make her fall in love with him. When she finally caved in and let him make love to her, discovering she was a virgin had stunned him, and he'd promised to marry her the way an honourable suitor would have.

Then he'd gone home to Florence to tell his family about her and it hadn't occurred to her once to wonder why, if he was serious about loving and marrying her, he hadn't taken her with him, as well. She'd just waited and waited like a fool for him to come back again. Long, empty days that had stretched into long, dragging weeks, and her only way to contact him had been via his mobile phone. She'd rung, she'd texted and eventually—after having her every message ignored—she'd finally received the painful hint that he didn't want anything more to do with her. So that last call she'd made to him eight long weeks later had really been a frightened cry for help.

And if she *ever* had to remind herself why she needed to hate Sandro then she'd just done it, Cassie told herself. Because even knowing now about his car accident and memory loss, she still would never forgive him for the brutal way he had cut her out of his life during that call.

Walking into work on Monday morning to find the way already smoothed for her by Ella's chatty mouth kept the cloud of normality hovering just above her head and she slipped comfortably into work mode. In fact, she went to great pains to present herself as the calm-mannered professional everyone at BarTec was used to seeing her as. She answered any questions tossed her way about Friday night—and there were plenty of them—with a cool humour that played the whole thing down until she let herself believe her curiosity value had died a quick death. She even managed to concentrate on some complicated financial projections and picked the phone up when it rang on her desk without thinking twice about who might be on the other end of the line.

So when Sandro's deep voice arrived in her ear she just froze in dismay. 'I am using Angus's old office,' he informed her coolly. 'I want to see you, Cassie. Now.'

'For goodness' sake,' she whispered fiercely into the mouthpiece, while slanting a hunted glance around the room to check if anyone was looking at her, 'I'm not coming anywhere near you in this building—or ever again, come to that!'

Ignoring that last part, 'Then I will come to your office,' he said.

'No!' She stood up so fast that she caught Ella's attention, the other girl's eyes opening wide in surprise at the abruptness with which she uttered that single negative. Fighting to get her voice under control, 'I'll be there straight away,' Cassie responded with only the barest bite of ice.

Refusing to look at anyone directly, including

Ella, she walked out of the office. Angus's old inner sanctum was situated behind the pair of double doors she could see directly in front her at the far end of the corridor, which meant she had to walk between two rows of glass-panelled offices beyond which anyone who was interested could witness the path she took. And that wasn't the end of her cheek-stinging journey because on the other side of the pair of doors was a large outer office where Angus's secretary had used to sit in peaceful isolation.

Now the poor woman was being forced to share her space with half a dozen of Sandro's team, each one of whom stopped what they were doing to stare at Cassie as she stepped through the door. It was like having to walk a line of a thousand curious eyes. She didn't have a clue as to what these particular people believed had taken place on Friday evening but the hum of their total silence buzzed like a wasp trapped against her eardrum.

Pinning a distant smile to her tense lips, she just kept on going, refusing to glance to her left or her right. She didn't even pause between her short knock and turning the handle to open the door which led the way to Sandro himself. However, trying to appear professional at all costs meant she was trembling inside by the time she'd closed the door behind her again, and anger was fizzing away in her blood.

At least he was alone, she saw, her sparking green gaze tracking across the room to where he stood behind Angus's old desk with his attention seemingly fixed on the view beyond the window. He was wearing another dark business suit that looked as if it had been tailored exclusively for him and the October sunlight was shining on the silk gloss of his hair.

An unwanted wash of physical awareness dragged on the tense muscles surrounding her abdomen, followed instantly by a sinking wash of shame. She'd been suffering from the same two sensations all weekend each time she caught herself thinking about him—the sexual drag, the sinking shame, usually joined by a thick lump of tears to block her throat. Only this time the constriction was due to tension not tears as she stood waiting for him to turn and acknowledge her presence.

But he didn't turn. As the silence stretched

between them Cassie began to wonder if he'd heard her come in the room.

Tugging some air into her lungs, 'I'm here on your time, Sandro,' she announced herself coolly.

'*Alessandro*,' he corrected without turning, 'when we are here anyway.'

Never. Her chin shot up in direct defiance of that comment. She was never going to refer to him by that name. She'd met him as Sandro. He had left her as Sandro. As far as she was concerned he'd come back into her life as Sandro, and until he came up with a good excuse as to why he'd lied to her about his name he was staying Sandro.

'I was in the middle of something important,' she informed him stiffly, 'and summoning me here like this is going to set the tongues wagging again. So if you would just tell me what you want, I would rather get out of here again as quickly as I can.'

'Feeling the strain?'

'Are you?' she threw right back at him.

He turned at that, the glimmer of a smile playing with the hard compression of his mouth.

'If that was your sweet way of asking me how I am feeling today, then the answer is lousy.'

'Oh,' Cassie said, disconcerted by that honest answer.

He looked it too, now he was letting her see his face. Oh, his undeniable good looks were all there in his clean, smooth, vibrant features, but his colour wasn't good and there was tension around his eyes which matched the tension she could see in his mouth.

'Come and sit down.' With a wave of a hand he invited her forward, and, because she was beginning to feel like an idiot hovering by the door, Cassie complied.

He watched her all the way, much as his team had watched her cross the outer office, but Sandro did it with his eyes half-hidden by the low droop of his eyelids that made her acutely aware of her grey tailored suit that had seen better days, and the prim way she'd stuck her hair in a knot at the back of her head.

Her eyes therefore sparked him a glance of cold challenge as she reached the chair set in front of the desk and sat down on it.

'You're angry with me,' he murmured.

'If you've brought me here to talk about… personal matters then you should not have done,' Cassie replied. 'I've spent the whole morning being as careful as I could be squashing curiosity about us. One phone call from you and I might as well have walked in here this morning and blasted out the whole truth.'

'But you didn't.'

'No.'

'In fact, you've played it very cool, from what I've been told. Apparently Angus plays a very big role in our…acquaintance.'

'Blame Jason Farrow for that,' she said. 'He's the one who put it about that both our fathers were friends with Angus.'

'He also told everyone I couldn't take my eyes off you all evening. He's been very busy.'

'He likes to believe he's more important than he is.'

'You don't like him.'

Lifting her cool gaze to meet his, she replied, 'Does it matter if I do or I don't?'

Sandro offered a shrug. 'Not really.'

'Then why are we having this conversation about him?'

'In an attempt to smooth your ruffled feathers before we move on to discuss you and me and the twins…?'

Cassie dropped her gaze as her icy composure cracked right down the middle because she just had not expected him to say that about the twins.

'There's nothing to discuss.' Staring down at her fingers where they lay on her lap, she watched them pleat together in a white-knuckled clench. 'They're my children. My responsibility.'

'You told me they were my children too,' Sandro reminded her.

'We both said a lot of things on Friday night that didn't add up to much worth remembering.'

She sensed the stinging whip of his irritation at her blocking tactics. With a shift of his stance that made her tense spine start to tingle, Cassie listened to his footsteps bring him around the desk until his black shoes appeared in front of her lowered gaze. There was a whisper of expensive clothing as he settled his thighs on the edge of the desk. Prickly heat feathered out from the sudden increased pace of her heartbeat when she breathed in his subtle, now dizzyingly familiar scent.

'Born on the fifteenth of January,' he dropped onto her very gently, adding the year and even the time of the twins' birth, 'a boy and a girl, each weighing five and a half pounds.'

Her startled green gaze shot upwards to clash head-on with steady dark brown. 'How did you find all of that out?' she demanded in gasping, shocked bewilderment.

And he might admit to feeling lousy but this close up he just looked gorgeous and sexy and disgustingly healthy.

'I spoke to Angus.'

Angus? 'Why would you want to drag him into this?'

'To find out anything I could about you and the twins without formally applying for information from the personnel department here?' he offered up in a smooth, mocking tone steeped in his own absolute justification.

Her cheeks stung hot with anger. 'You had no right to go anywhere to dig into my business.'

'Are you telling me now that the twins are not mine?'

Biting back the desire to lie, Cassie lowered her eyes and said nothing.

'Wise of you, *cara*,' Sandro drawled. 'For I might be suffering from memory loss but my intelligence is still intact. I can do simple arithmetic. I can even count backwards on my fingers nine months.'

'The twins were premature—'

'By two weeks,' he confirmed the shocking depth of his new knowledge. 'I managed to incorporate it into my calculations. Not bad for a guy who spent his weekend reeling from one knock-out memory flash to another—all of which still placed you in the starring role.'

'So what do you want—my sympathy?' Cassie shot at him, lancing up off the chair and onto her feet.

It was a stupid mistake to make because she found herself standing almost toe to toe with him again, and because his hips rested against the desk, their eyes were level—dark and deep and swirling with the turbulent reflection of his present feelings.

'No,' he said, 'I just want to hear *you* confirm the truth to me.'

Cassie went to turn away from him but he turned her back again, his hand arriving on her arm to achieve that aim. She tried a tug to free it, but he held on and the moment his fingers made contact with the skin at her wrist things started to happen inside her she did not want to feel.

'I h-hate you, Sandro,' she breathed tensely.

'I can see that you do,' he responded dryly, 'which is why you are trembling and your body heat is altering, and your soft lips are pulsing as they fill with warm, sensual blood. Friday night I wanted to rip your dress off and toss you down on the nearest flat surface long before I actually got around to doing it. I was so hot for you my head burned. I ploughed this really strange course between crazed confusion and sexual madness and the two only merged together when I held you naked beneath me in my bed with your hungry mouth fixed on mine.'

Cassie tossed her head back. 'Are you so proud of the way you behaved that you're this happy to describe it?'

She watched, astonished, as two streaks of colour shot high across his cheeks. 'I lost control,' he confessed. 'I apologise if I was too—passionate.'

Too passionate? In her estimation they'd both been *too passionate*. Hot, wild, out of their...

'I should have apologised to you directly afterwards, but you'd knocked me for six again and I never got around to it.'

'I don't want your apology.' Feeling as if she was being eaten alive by her own culpability that night, Cassie gave another tug at her captured arm and this time managed to pull free and step right out of reach. 'And I've already told you I don't want to have this kind of conversation with you here.'

'Have dinner with me tonight, then,' he invited. 'We can talk on neutral ground.'

'No.' With an abrupt twist she headed for the door.

His sigh of irritation trembled down her backbone. 'Saturday, then,' he offered. 'I have to go away tomorrow and cannot get back to London until the weekend. Cassie, *don't* walk out of that door before we reach a compromise here!' he warned. 'I want to meet my children, and I prefer to do it with your permission and blessing but I will meet them without both if you force me to!'

Cassie whipped around. 'Are you threatening

me?' she choked out, taut and trembling with a frantic mix of anger and alarm.

A scowl wrecked the shape of his attractive mouth. 'No—' springing up from the desk like some lithe hunting animal annoyed by the self-built cage of his own response '—not unless I have to,' he temporised.

In other words he was threatening her! Cassie wrapped her arms around her middle, crushing the fabric of her grey suit jacket against her ribs. She wanted to call his bluff and tell him to get lost but she knew she couldn't. She just didn't possess that much power over the truth. And the truth was—love it or hate it—Sandro was the father of her children. If he wanted to meet them, what right did she have to throw obstacles in his way? She couldn't do that to the twins or to him. Her own feelings couldn't come into it. They—the three of them—had a given right to know each other even if it meant she had to put her own grievances with Sandro aside in order to make it happen.

But what was it going to mean to her to have Sandro stroll in and out of her life at his leisure? To see him interact with the two people she loved beyond anything else in the world?

Watching her stand there fighting a battle with herself scraped at the inner walls of Sandro's chest. He knew this was tough on her. He knew she would rather slap his face again and tell him to go to hell. He'd left her. He'd walked away to leave her to cope on her own. He'd rejected her in the most brutal way a man could do it. *I don't know you. I don't want to know you. Please don't ring this number again...* Those words had been eating him up since she'd quoted them back to him. It didn't matter that he could not remember having said them. The point was he *had* to have said them. He didn't dare let himself wonder what she must have felt like to be on the receiving end of such brutality.

A spark of pain sent his fingers up to rub at his brow. He needed to remember but all he kept getting were these flashes that seared through his head, only to lock him out again.

'I want to meet them, Cassie,' he repeated determinedly.

'Three nights ago you didn't even know you had two children!' she cried out painfully. 'You can't even remember me! N-no,' she refused yet again, trying desperately to control her shaking voice, 'not yet at least, n-not until I can be sure...'

'Be sure of what?' he prompted when the rest dried on her tongue.

Cassie pulled in a breath. 'Be sure that you m-mean to stay around for them.'

'And you don't think I will?'

Lowering her eyes, she just shrugged and said nothing.

'On what evidence do you make this judgement of my character?' he demanded haughtily.

Was he joking? No, he wasn't, she saw by his taut, proud stance. 'Since you're the man I spent two weeks with and didn't see again for six years, I don't know how you dare stand there and say that.'

'And you hold this against me though I've explained the circumstances?'

Yes, that was exactly what she was saying, Cassie had to concede. 'Look.' She sighed, accepting that he had a point. 'I just think it's too soon to bring the twins into this. They're so young and vulnerable, Sandro! Letting you walk into their lives because you're curious about them and because you feel you have the right to do it does not—'

'So at least you accept that I do possess the right!'

Moistening her lips, Cassie nodded. 'But I

think you need more time to consider what it's going to mean to your life *before* you decide to meet them.'

'If they are my children then I don't need to take time to decide anything,' he declared stiffly.

'If,' Cassie picked up. *'If* they're your children? You see, you *don't* really even know for sure!'

It was stalemate. He knew it, Cassie knew it. Releasing a hard sigh of frustration, he lifted a hand up to rub at his brow.

Cassie watched tensely as the colour began to drain from his face. It was happening again, and the aching thrum of concern for him began to war with her need to maintain her defences against him. She was scared of what he could do to her, scared of this man called Alessandro Marchese because of the power he possessed over the most important things in her life—her children and her job. Sandro Rossi had been a different person. Younger, way less intimidating because he had not worn the hard shell of maturity and the aura of power and inner strength she was seeing now, despite the physical weakness presently troubling him.

And she was even more scared of how he could make her feel. Even now her muscles were twitching with a need to go back across the room to him, her heart thumping heavy and slow in her chest because…because no matter which name he went by there was this fine-wire link of intimacy at work between them, tugging so strongly on her emotions that in the end she had to give in to it.

Walking back to him, she reached up to touch the back of his hand. 'OK?' she questioned huskily.

'*Sí,*' he responded.

Lips trembling, she parted them to take in a small breath before asking, 'Have you remembered anything over the weekend?'

Sandro gave a shake of his head. 'Nothing I can hold on to before it is gone again.'

'Did—did you see your…your brother, the doctor, again?'

Compressed mouth stretching into a smile, he lowered his hand and Cassie found herself drowning in the rueful glow in his dark eyes. 'I know what's wrong with me, Cassie—my memory is trying to return to me. What can any doctor do other than to advise me to be patient and expose myself as much as possible to the trigger that's helping me to remember? You and I both know that you are that trigger.' Reaching up, he touched a gentle finger to the corner of her mouth. 'Your face, your hair, your sparkling green eyes, your smooth, slender body and this soft, quivering mouth I want to lean in and kiss so badly that I'm aching again.'

The last part made Cassie blink then take a jerky step backwards. Watching her do it brought back his wry smile.

'No kindly offer to help me out here?' he quizzed. 'A more charitable woman would lean in and kiss me, if only for experiment.'

'Who is Sandro Rossi?' The question arrived right out of the middle of the hot cloud of temptation Cassie found she was bathed in.

'Ah.' He grimaced. 'Were you always this heartless?'

'I can't remember,' she shot back. 'You tell me.'

'I will one day, I promise you.'

'So who is Sandro Rossi?' she repeated firmly, wishing…wishing she could just turn and walk away from him but she couldn't, for he was, bottom line, the father of her children and nothing was ever going to change that, whatever name he used.

'I am Sandro Rossi,' he announced, 'Alessandro Giancola Marchese Rossi,' he extended like a sensually loaded introduction that plied melting heat along Cassie's bones. 'It is a family thing. Alessandro comes from my paternal grandfather. My grandmother brought the Marchese name into the family along with the Marchese wealth and power.'

Reaching into his inside jacket pocket, he produced two cards which he handed to Cassie. One was clearly a business card bearing the Marchese logo above the shortened name *Alessandro Marchese* along with the usual contact details. The other card brought a lump to her throat because she recognised it as similar to the one he had given to her six years ago. It was simply scribed with the name *Alessandro Rossi*.

'I did not lie to you, Cassie,' he stated quietly. 'I am so used to having two names that I rarely bother to think about it. The Rossi family was not poor but it could not match the Marchese wealth and power. When my great-grandfather married his only child off to a Rossi, he insisted that all first-born sons thereafter must have Marchese included in their name and adopt it when the time came for them to inherit. I inherited the name when my father died two years ago. Until then I still called myself a Rossi....'

Eyes stinging now as she stared down at the cards held in her fingers, Cassie thought about Anthony, Sandro's first-born son. 'Now you've broken with tradition.'

'*Sí*, I have broken with tradition.'

'And the other name you mentioned?' Her eyelashes trembled as she looked up at him and saw a rueful kind of smile touch his attractive mouth.

'Giancola brings together two uncles, Gianni and Nicola—my father's brothers—in respect of their memory...they died at birth...' As if he couldn't stop himself from doing it, Sandro reached up to gently comb a stray lock of hair from her cheek. 'They were twins, *cara*. See how the pieces begin to fit together?'

Some, she agreed, but not all of them. 'Pandora told me that you hate being called Sandro, yet you introduced yourself to me by that name.'

To her surprise he uttered a short laugh. 'It's a

strange phenomenon that makes sense to me only now that I've met you again. Pandora was telling the truth—I have hated hearing myself called Sandro for years…six years to be exact,' he added ironically. 'Then you arrive back in my life, spitting Sandro at me, and it all began to make a crazy kind of sense.'

'To you perhaps but not to me.'

'I might have holes in my memory where you are concerned, *cara*, but I must have maintained a pretty powerful link with you through the use of that name. No one else is allowed to use it without earning my anger, yet I love to hear you use it. Think about it,' he urged. 'It's been a six-year trigger just waiting to happen.'

'And may never have happened but for a chance meeting in a restaurant bar,' Cassie tagged on, placing a dampener on the power he seemed to be applying to the use of a name.

She offered the cards back to him but he refused to take them. 'Keep them in case you need to call me.'

The icy shiver of *déjà vu* that lanced down her spine was an even more powerful trigger to Cassie. Maybe he realised it because he breathed out a short sigh. 'My mobile phone was in my pocket on the day I had the accident. I did not see or touch it again until I was fit and able to start work again. I did not intentionally ignore your calls.'

But he had to have picked up those missed calls eventually, Cassie extended silently. Had he assumed that she was some kind of nutcase calling him because by then he did not remember her? If so then by the time she made her last frantic call he was ready for her; *I don't know you. I don't want to know you. Please don't call this number again.*

'I'm sorry I was so brutal with you,' he murmured, seemingly able to read her mind when he couldn't even read his own. 'I wish I could remember doing it—I feel I deserve to remember being so brutal.' His hand lifted up to cover his frowning brow again. 'But I promise you I will never let it happen again.'

Fine words, Cassie thought, knowing she had to accept them because—what other choice did she have? She could continue to resent him to hell and back for his cruel rejection but he would always remain the father of her children.

Nothing, not even an apology, was going to change that.

So, pressing her lips together, she just nodded and closed her fingers around the contact cards then turned and walked back to the door. As she reached it she paused, the uneven beat of her aching heart telling her what she was going to do next before she had even formed the words.

'I'm going to visit Angus on Saturday,' she announced with an unsteady thickness. 'Perhaps you could turn up there too. Th-the twins love it there... I can let them loose to run wild in Angus's garden... It—it's as neutral a place I can think of for the three of you to m-meet.'

'*Sí*... Yes... Thank you,' Sandro responded with a rough catch in his voice.

Cassie stared down at her shoes. 'Their names are...'

'I know their names, *cara*,' he inserted gruffly, 'Anthony and Isabelle....'

Cassie nodded. 'Sh-she—Isabelle prefers to be called Bella,' she managed to push past the constriction trying to strangle her throat. 'Bella was born first, three minutes before her brother. Th-the Bella name stuck because—because it was the way Anthony first said her name, whereas he…' She had to stop to swallow. She wasn't facing him but she knew he wasn't moving a single muscle and tears were pushing at the backs of her eyes now. 'H-he's always Anthony because Bella never had trouble saying his name. But then…but then Bella is like that, sh-she's sharp and quick and— Have a good trip and we'll see you on Saturday.'

Unable to hang around here for another heart-wrenching second of this, Cassie found herself standing on the other side of his office door experiencing her second sense of *déjà vu* in as many minutes—this one spinning her back to the restaurant on Friday night.

The big difference this time being that she now found herself standing here with her composure shot to pieces and staring at a room full of curious eyes instead of a thankfully empty space. She felt her face drain of colour, her eyes moving on what felt like guilty wings to focus on the narrow-eyed glitter spitting out from the black eyes of Pandora Batiste.

Guilty fire came to lick up her neck to burn a mortified path to her cheeks. If the other woman was Sandro's lover then she had every right to pin her to the door with a look like that, Cassie accepted. Did she know—*could* Pandora know what she and Sandro had done on Friday night?

Telephones suddenly started ringing—half a dozen of them bursting simultaneously into life. Watching smart-suited people jump to their workstations, Cassie took her chance while she had it and hurried across the room. As she slipped out through the door she heard a cumulative murmur of, '*Sí, Alessandro,*' and almost felt the backlash as a dozen or so bodies made a mass move towards Sandro's office door.

He'd done it to divert their attention away from her, she realised with a small laugh that deteriorated into a strangled choke.

CHAPTER SEVEN

'HE'S very good with them, don't you think?'

'Yes.' Cassie nodded, wishing she knew whether to laugh or to weep, as she watched Sandro go down in a huddle on the lawn in his bungled attempt to stop the ball Bella had just kicked into his improvised goal area, marked by two anoraks provided by the twins.

Bella certainly found it hilariously funny because she was jumping up and down and squealing with delight as the ball rolled right past him, setting Anthony running to go and catch it.

The afternoon was bright and sunny but way too cool to tempt Angus outside. Electing to stay inside with him, the two of them now sat by the French windows with Angus occupying his favourite chair that Sandro had carried there so he could watch the children play. Seated on a low stool beside him, Cassie leant forward so she could rest her chin on the heels of her hands.

All in, she'd had a pretty lousy week, she reflected bleakly. Monday she'd felt wrecked by her confrontation with Sandro. Tuesday she'd felt wrecked by the discovery that Pandora Batiste was the real new boss Sandro had put in Angus's place. Sandro should not have even been at BarTec on Monday. The fact that he'd arrived there and commandeered Angus's office—which was now Pandora's office, apparently—exclusively to be private with Cassie had gone down with Pandora like a lead balloon.

By the end of Wednesday she knew she'd made a serious enemy in Pandora Batiste. She'd been hauled in front of the other woman to defend her commitment to the company. Her timekeeping had been called into question, and why she felt she had the right to finish work half an hour earlier than anyone else. When she'd explained that she took half an hour less at lunchtime to compensate, Pandora wasn't impressed. Did she know she took more holiday breaks than her colleagues? Was she aware that said extra holidays were not a part of her employment contract with BarTec? A verbal agreement with Angus that she could catch up by working from home during school breaks did not suit her new boss, who, she was told, did not approve of unequal favours built on the flimsy excuse of verbal agreements. When she promised to make new arrangements for collecting and caring for her children Pandora still wasn't pleased.

Not once was Sandro's name mentioned, but his spectre wove in and out of each criticism she was forced to take on the chin. She spent Thursday mostly on the phone trying to fill in the half-hour gap between the twins leaving school and her being able to collect them and did not dare to even try to think about the half-term break due in a couple of weeks. By Friday she knew she was in serious trouble when she arrived at BarTec to discover that her every working moment was to be shadowed by one of Sandro's team.

Ella spent the day trying to bully her into telling Sandro what Pandora was doing but Cassie would rather have cut out her tongue than sneak to Sandro about it. Her pride had taken enough of a beating from Pandora.

And all because of this man, who was playing with her children as if he'd always been there for them.

'He told you everything before we arrived, didn't he?' she murmured flatly to Angus.

'It is in his nature to meet uncomfortable issues head-on,' her father's old friend supplied.

Not with me, thought Cassie.

'Look at the way he faced the twins when you arrived,' Angus highlighted. 'No playing it cagey, he just went straight in there.'

Sliding her fingers up to hide the revealing wobble suddenly attacking her mouth, Cassie closed her eyes in pained reflection of that heart-wrenching moment when Sandro had stood in this same room, and faced his children for the first time.

Wearing jeans and a soft grey jumper over an open-neck shirt, he'd looked so fabulously tall, dark, handsome…and so alarmingly tense and pale she'd feared he was going to drop to the floor in one of his blackouts.

'Sandro…' she'd murmured, unable to keep her concern hidden.

'I'm OK,' he'd husked out, but the way he

could not keep the unevenness from his voice told her otherwise. So had the blacker than black eyes he'd locked on the twins, who'd come to a standstill halfway across the room, the happy way they'd run in here to go straight to Angus, stunted by their surprise at being confronted with a stranger.

And no one, not Cassie, not Angus, who observed all from his chair, not even two five-year-olds, missed the tension holding Sandro, or the way he'd burned lingering looks from one twin to the other, seeing what Cassie already knew was there.

One green-eyed, golden-haired little girl and one dark-eyed, dark-haired little boy—two miniature replicas of their parents.

Cassie's throat closed on a lump of agony. At that point she would have given anything not to put the three of them through this. She'd watched Sandro swallow, watched him lift his eyes up to meet with hers, felt the ferocious sweep of emotion crash into her because he exposed so much vulnerability in that short, strained, heart-stopping glance.

'Anthony, Bella...' she'd tried her best to ease it for him '...this is Alessandro. S-say hello...'

The twins' obedient responses had been mumbled. A muscle running along the rigid edge of Sandro's jaw jerked as he'd looked back at them. Like a guy fighting a mammoth battle with himself he'd fought to place a smile on his mouth as he dropped into a squat in front of the two children.

Then he'd knocked Cassie sideways with his, 'Hello. I am your father. I am sorry we have not met before now…'

'It was quite courageous, considering.' Angus spoke beside her.

Considering what? Cassie wondered as sharp tears sliced across her eyes. 'A considerate man would have warned me he was going to announce it like that instead of just dropping it on the twins like a bomb.'

'A considerate woman would perhaps have prepared her children to expect it to come.'

Cassie flushed, tensing up at what she read as a criticism of her mothering instincts. 'I was hoping to give them breathing space between meeting Sandro and learning who he really is,' she defended her own reasoning.

Doing it Sandro's way had turned a simple first meeting into an emotional storm the likes of which she had never seen her children display. Bella had burst into a flood of wild tears. 'But we don't need a daddy!' she'd sobbed.

'And we don't want you as one!' Anthony had tagged on, his arm going around his twin in a fiercely protective gesture that said it all as far as the little boy was concerned.

'I never, not once, realised just how dreadfully vulnerable they felt about having no father,' Cassie confided with Angus.

'Alessandro was vulnerable too, Cassie,' Angus pointed out. 'He was as close to tears as you and Bella.'

It had been a horrible few seconds when nobody could find a thing to say that might have taken the edge off his distress. Bella kept on sobbing and Cassie had gone to hug her. Anthony had just stood glaring at Sandro while Sandro looked helplessly back.

'I'm amazed now that I never noticed the likeness before,' Angus put in thoughtfully.

'Why should you?' Cassie asked. 'You didn't know Sandro and I had even met each other.'

'Anthony has his father's hair and eyes and features, and his intense personality,' Angus said, 'as Bella possesses your golden beauty and fiery nature.'

'I'm not fiery!' she protested. In fact, she'd always believed herself to be a very calm and placid person—except with Sandro, of course, she was forced to acknowledge. Where he was concerned she—

'And he seemed to know instinctively how to handle them.'

Yes, he'd just taken control of his own emotions, reached out and gently taken Bella out of Cassie's arms, turned the little girl around and encouraged her to weep on his shoulder. When Anthony aimed a kick at him for touching his sister, he'd ignored the kick, smiled at his son then held out his free hand to him.

And Anthony had taken the hand, Cassie recalled as the lump in her throat, which had rarely been missing since she'd witnessed that wrenching little scene, thickened some more. Sandro had lowered himself into a chair still holding Bella against him, drawing a reluctant Anthony towards him until the small boy stood glowering at him from his wooden stance by Sandro's thigh. Then he'd talked to them. He'd talked and he'd talked in his low, soft accented voice that held the two children totally engrossed and turned Cassie's emotions inside out.

'He doesn't even remember me,' she whispered to Angus, unwittingly revealing how much that little truth hurt.

'No...' Angus sounded thoughtful. 'Human instinct is a fascinating thing when you think about it. He doesn't remember you yet he looks at you as if you are already his wife.'

His wife? Cassie shot to her feet on a surge of new-found energy. 'I don't know what it is you're cooking up in your head, Angus,' she said sternly, 'but I can tell you straight, I am not going to *marry* him!'

Her father's old friend smiled one of those I-know-you-better-than-you-know-yourself kind of smiles that softened some of the ravages of his illness out of his thin face. 'Fiery, as I said.'

Ignoring that, 'Has Sandro mentioned this marriage thing to you?' she demanded sharply.

Making a gesture with one of his long, frail, bony hands, 'That's something you will have to take up with him, not with me,' he replied.

Not while I live and breathe, thought Cassie,

frowning fiercely because she couldn't understand why she was getting so het up about something that just was not going to be. Unsettled,
restless now, unhappy about the feelings
suddenly running around inside her, she glanced
at her watch.

'It's time for us to leave if we want to catch our
train,' she mumbled, turning towards the French
windows with the intention of calling in the twins.

'Running away, Cassie?' Angus said gently.
'Perhaps you are living with the badly mistaken
fear that the man you see out there playing with
his children is going to disappear out of your
lives as quickly as he came into them.'

Her shoulders tensed. 'He did it once.'

'Due to a car accident that came at a very in-
opportune time for the two of you,' Angus
pointed out. 'Now here you both are, being given
an opportunity to put right something which
perhaps would not have happened if Alessandro
had not been so…incapacitated. Think about it,
Cassie. Fate does not hand out these chances so
often that you can afford to pass them by because
you are feeling hurt by what you still think of as
his desertion.'

'Forgive and forget?' She laughed, a glimpse of her old dry humour creeping out. 'Perhaps I need a knock on the head, then, to help even things out a bit between us!'

Angus laughed too. 'Meeting him halfway would be much less painful.'

Meet him halfway over what though? The twins? Well, she'd already accepted she had to do that for their sake.

'If it helps, I think your father would have approved of him.'

Turning round, Cassie walked back to Angus and leant down to press a kiss against his cool, bony cheek. 'Stop playing Cupid for your own amusement,' she scolded, then added more softly, 'And you look tired, so we're going to leave before you exhaust yourself trying to soften me up for Sandro.'

But Sandro didn't need Angus to champion his cause because he'd found two much better candidates for the role—as she discovered ten seconds later when the French windows suddenly flew open to let the twins run inside along with a gust of cool air.

'Guess what, Uncle Angus,' Bella announced, 'our mummy and daddy are going to get married!'

'And we're all going to live in Italy!' Anthony tagged on.

Having spun around in time to catch the excited glow on the twins' faces, Cassie raised her eyes to meet with Sandro's steady gaze and just froze.

He'd planned all of this with the precision of an army general. She could see it declared right there in the cool expression stamped on his face. He'd taken the neutral ground she'd offered him for this meeting at Angus's home and invaded it before she'd even got here. Then he'd moved on to phase two, by wooing the twins into accepting him as their father, then wooed them some more with what must amount to them as the solid gold prize!

Marriage—a real family unit. A home together in an exciting new place. And he'd mapped it all out for the twins during an improvised game of football played out on Angus's lawn.

Clever, smooth, stunningly slick, she allowed him as she continued to stand there taking in his supremely relaxed almost arrogant stance, while the twins shot past her to go and lean on the arms of Angus's chair. They were telling him everything, though Cassie barely listened. They were ordering him to hurry up and get well so he could come and visit them in Italy. And throughout this minor commotion they were creating, Sandro did not let his gaze drop from hers.

Sandro suspected that if they'd been alone she would be issuing another hit to his face. He'd outmanoeuvred and trapped her before she'd been aware there was a trap to be sprung.

Marriage. 'The only answer,' he announced under cover of the twins' excited chatter.

He watched her lips part and quiver. He watched the ice in her eyes melt to a dull shade of green. Hurt, he recognised with a twinge of remorse which still did not touch his resolve. 'Next week,' he extended. 'Arrangements are already in place for a quiet civil ceremony here in London. We will do the proper wedding thing later, once we are…settled as a family.'

'Why?' she breathed.

Breaking his lock on her eyes, instead of answering he flicked a glance towards Angus. Like a puppet pulled by the younger man's strings, the older man rose up from his chair and led the twins out of the room on the promise of a snack before they had to leave.

The silence their departure left behind hung around Cassie's throat like a noose. Sandro moved away from the French windows to place the twins' coats down on a chair then turned back to face her. The cool breeze outside had blanched his skin of some of its warm colour and she could smell the fresh air still permeating his clothes. Like herself, he was wearing casual jeans and a sweater, the difference being that his outfit was designer quality whereas hers was made up from the cheapest high-street bargains she could find. But then everything about Sandro was like that, she mused bleakly—designed to impress: his dominating height, the undeniable physical attraction built into his long, masculine framework, the silky blackness of his hair even when it had been ruffled by a breeze, and the stunning bone structure that made up his too-handsome face. Naked he looked fabulous, dressed he looked fabulous—but did the quality of the inner man match the quality of the outer shell?

No. Inside he was a sneaky, conniving, ruthless operator with his attention concentrated solely on himself. On what *he* wanted. On what he decided suited *him*.

Folding her arms tight across her slender ribcage, 'Talk to me or I walk,' she threatened when he still made no effort to justify what he'd done.

'No, you won't,' he countered evenly. 'You're too committed to putting the twins' feelings before your own.'

The fact that she knew he was right about that did not make Cassie feel less hostile towards him. 'Is that why you set me up like this?'

'Backed you into a tight corner?' He dared to arch one of those super-smooth black eyebrows. 'Of course.' He added a super-smooth shrug. 'You would have fought me to hell and back otherwise. Unfold your arms, *cara*,' he went off track to instruct as he walked towards her. 'You look like a fisherman's wife ready to go on the warpath.'

She'd barely breathed a gasp of protest before he'd done it for her, reaching out and taking hold of her forearms and urging them to part.

'I want my children legally bound to me, and I want you,' he declared without releasing her arms from his grasp. 'We could have spent weeks…months creeping around the subject of marriage; now it is done. You can be as mad with me as you want to be but we both know you won't attempt to change a thing if it means upsetting the twins. You gave them a father today, *cara*…' his voice deepened to husky '…now you must accept the consequences of your—generosity. So we marry next week.' He even named the date and the venue. 'Then we go to Florence to live.'

'And does your mistress come along with us?' Her acid response flew right out of the centre of her burning frustration because he'd hit her with too many inarguable truths.

Sandro looked at her curiously. 'Does this very fortunate woman have a name?'

Fortunate…? Cassie tried to pull free of him but he refused to let her. 'Everyone at BarTec knows Pandora Batiste is your lover— Let go of me,' she bit out.

'Pandora is my lover?' His dark eyes began to gleam, the sensuous shape of his mouth daring to stretch into a grin. 'I must warn her to be discreet from now on, then.'

Cassie rose to the bait without thinking about it; wrenching an arm free, she threw the flat of her palm at his face! Only this time Sandro was ready for her. He caught the hand before it had a chance to make contact with its target, his long fingers gently imprisoning her tense fingers, the golden flecks in his eyes spinning out a warning into spitting, sparking, icy green as he used her captured hand to tug her closer. Shutting down the space between their two bodies he brought his mouth down onto hers.

An angry kiss was a dangerous kiss, she discovered two seconds later when she went into it like the fisherman's wife he'd just accused her of being, squirming and fighting him and kissing him back as if she'd been dying to do it for days. When he let go of her captured wrist so he could wrap his arms around her she attacked him with her nails, clawing them down the length of his back and making him heave out a shuddering curse yet arch his body into her so she felt the full power of his burgeoning response. His hands gripped her slender hip bones, holding her clamped against him, his tongue exploring her mouth. When he decided to pull back from her the desperate need to wound him somehow sent her teeth scoring the inner tissue of his lower lip.

'You little witch,' he gasped, eyes glinting like gold fires transmitting his surprise.

'I hate you!' Cassie seared at him feverishly.

'You want me,' he translated. 'And—*per Dio*—you are going to have me night after night after night once I get you safely hitched to me!'

'With the *fortunate* Pandora to supplement your daytime needs?'

'That is up to you. Will I need her?' He was still touching his lip with a careful finger. 'And who the hell taught you to be such an aggressive kisser?' he raked out. 'It damn well wasn't me.'

'How do you know that it wasn't you?' Cassie countered.

It happened again like a thunderbolt tossed at his rock-solid jaw. His head went back. He tensed up all over, his eyes turning into deep black holes in his head as he took a step back from her then staggered.

Seeing what was coming, Cassie cried out on the sharp edge of alarm when she thought he was going to drop to the floor the way he'd done twice before. 'Sandro—*don't*—!'

With an impressive shift of his reeling body, he ensured Angus's chair took his weight with a shudder. With no awareness as to how she had arrived there, Cassie was on her knees between his spread thighs. 'Sandro,' she murmured, one of her hands already covering the racing beat of his heart.

'I'm OK.' His fingers were at his brow again. 'I've got it…covered.'

But he wasn't OK! 'This has got to stop happening!' she burst out. 'Every time we get confrontational you almost black out on me!'

'I'm a big boy, *cara*. I can take confrontation without blacking out.'

'Then what the heck triggered it this time?'

He released an odd laugh. 'Could be the mind-blowing way you kissed me,' Sandro suggested, still struggling to deal with the real trigger that had almost knocked him to the floor this time, 'which is going to make ours an interesting marriage.'

'Shut up about marriage.' Frowning fiercely now, unable to stop her other hand from reaching up to touch her fingers against the worrying clammy skin covering his cheek, she added, 'You shouldn't have brought the subject up at all. If you ask me we shouldn't even occupy the same room!'

'No comment about your kissing technique, then.'

The lid almost blew off Cassie's temper. Only the sight of his dreadful pallor kept the lid on. His eyes were still closed, the skin covering his face drawn tight across the bones, and she was worried and scared, her insides were churning around like mad and he was turning it into a joke!

Sitting back on her heels, Cassie released a tense breath. 'You've got as much sensitivity as a doorstop.'

On a sigh, he dropped his hand and opened his eyes to pin her with an inky black stare of dead certainty. 'We are getting married.'

'Why?' she cried out. 'Because of the twins?'

'Because we both know that marriage between us has to be the logical solution, so you tell me, why do you feel the need to fight against it?'

The answer to that was simple. 'You don't even know me.'

'I know myself and I know I would have been there for you and the twins from the beginning if I had not had the accident and lost my memory. Marriage between us would have been an essential part of that.'

Would it? Cassie wasn't sure.

Getting to her feet, she paced away from him, that inner core of uncertainty nagging at her as she walked. Swinging around, 'Tell me,' she said, 'who else did you forget about in your missing weeks?'

'No one—that I know of.' He frowned at her. 'What has that got to do with anything?'

'Hasn't it occurred to you to wonder why your brain singled me out to wipe from your head?'

His frowned deepened. 'Probably because you are the only person I met for the first time during those weeks.' Fingers going up to rub at his brow again, he sat forward on the chair. 'I don't see that it matters.'

Well, it mattered to Cassie. 'I could be anyone, then. I could be feeding you a pack of lies, for all you know.'

He dropped the hand. 'Why would you want to do that?'

'Money?' she suggested. 'The pot of gold from the filthy-rich man? Security for my children?'

Sandro suddenly launched to his feet. 'Don't try telling me they are not my children!'

'I'm not!' she denied, tensing up all over

because she didn't like the way he swayed before he gained control of his stance. 'But without a chance meeting in a restaurant bar last week, you could have lived the rest of your life not knowing the twins and I even existed! And are you sure, Sandro—can you be positively certain that they are yours? If I were in your shoes I would be demanding DNA tests to make sure before I committed myself to anything.'

He uttered a thick laugh. 'You sound like my legal advisors.'

'So they've said the same thing?' Cassie picked up. 'Have they also advised you to have me investigated?'

He sighed impatiently. 'I might not remember you but I do *know* you,' he insisted. 'There's this…link between us which keeps on lighting up inside my head that tells me I know you, though it will not stay around long enough for me to capture it thoroughly.'

'You might be catching brief glimpses of a clever gold-digger, for all you know—a greedy little scrubber with an eye on the main chance!'

'I might have gaps in my memory but not in my intelligence,' he threw back. 'I still possess the ability to recognise greedy little scrubbers when I set eyes on them. And you are not one of them.'

'Then what other reason can you come up with for making me the only person you've wiped out of your head?'

A strange expression crossed his face before he blanked it out with a hiss of impatience. 'I don't understand why you are obsessing about this.'

'Because it hurts!' Cassie flung at him. '*I* don't understand it, and it *hurts*! And I won't let you talk me into a marriage with you, Sandro, when I will be constantly waiting for your memory to come back and *tell* you why you needed to forget me!'

In the sizzling silence that followed her outburst, if it was possible his face bleached even paler than it already was. Cassie could feel his stress, his simmering tension. And that scary blank look was back in his eyes, as if he was remembering something else. She watched him fight with it, watched his eyelids fold downwards to half cover the look with a tense black frown that made her hold on to her breath because she knew—just knew he was about to tell her something so devastating to her it was going to rip her to shreds.

A sound coming from the other side of the living-room door warned them then that the twins were about to come back in here. Sandro's curse as he pushed his hand back up to his face cut through the tension like a knife.

'I'll h-head them off.' Cassie jerked into movement, making for the door on knocking knees and trembling legs.

'Give me a few minutes to…get myself together,' he husked out. 'Then I will take you home.'

'We'll catch the train—'

'Don't,' he growled, 'start that argument again. I will take you,' he insisted. 'Find my driver. He can usually be found out by the garages, drinking tea with Angus's driver.'

That he had not driven himself here swung Cassie round in surprise. Sandro was still on his feet but only just, she judged anxiously as she watched the way he flexed his wide shoulders as if he was trying to shake off what was affecting him, and a sudden ribbon of understanding slithered down her front. He didn't trust himself to drive a car right now while these blackouts kept on catching him out.

Moistening her lips, her heart thumping, she heard the husky concern shadowing her voice. 'Sandro, you—'

The door flew open, forcing whatever she had been going to say back down her throat, and sent her attention zipping away from him to the twins. With the efficiency of a mother used to dealing with two boisterous children, she herded them back out of the room before they could lay eyes on their father, diverting them with the tempting promise that they were about to travel home in style instead of catching a busy train.

Sandro waited until the door had closed behind them before he dropped back down into the chair then reached into his pocket for his mobile phone. 'Marco,' he said brusquely, 'I'm giving in. I will take that scan now....'

CHAPTER EIGHT

THE journey back home was completed in an atmosphere of strange, tense, chattering normality, made to work because Sandro had elected to take the seat beside his driver, which left space in the rear of the car for Cassie and the twins. The two children were so impressed by this luxury mode of transport that they did not notice their father's silence or the quiet tension threading their mother's husky voice whenever she spoke to them.

He declined her invitation to come in with them. On one level Cassie was relieved because she knew she needed time out of his dominating sphere. On another level she ached with concern for him because he still looked so strained and pale.

He smiled for the twins, though, promised to come and see them again soon. He squatted down on the dusty pavement so he could look them directly in their eyes as he made the promise then remained like that, drinking in their solemn little faces as if for the last time. Then Bella stepped in and wrapped her arms around his neck, and Sandro reached out to loop a big arm around his son to draw him into the hug too.

Why this touching little scene should fill Cassie with fresh anxiety she couldn't work out, but when he rose to his full height and turned that same intense look on her she almost copied her daughter and threw herself at him. The way he cupped her cheek and brushed his thumb across her soft, trembling mouth stopped her. His husky, 'I'll call you,' before he turned and climbed back in the car without saying anything else left her feeling wrung out and devastated because he'd used the exact same words and touch when he'd driven away from her six years ago.

She spent Sunday living with that empty feeling, while the twins plied her with non-stop questions about their father and marriage plans and Sandro's proposed move to Italy, about which she knew nothing. Bella was excited about it. Anthony worried about leaving his school and his friends. Cassie lived in an anxious state over Sandro and that final scene on the pavement, which grew more sickeningly familiar each time she replayed it in her head.

And he didn't call.

Monday she turned up for work and made the pretence it was like any other Monday morning with no major upheaval happening in her life—because she just didn't know what else to do. Her shadow followed her every moment, helping to keep her concentration focused on work. But she was uptight and uncommunicative, alert for the sound of Sandro's name being mentioned, wondering if he was in the building, wanting to find out, reassure herself that he was OK, but refusing to give herself the right to ask those questions outright.

And then there was Pandora. She did not seem to be in the building either, although that was yet another question Cassie refused to seek confirmation about.

Tuesday went the same way as Monday. By Wednesday Sandro's contact cards had found their way out of her purse and now burned a hole in the slanted pocket of her pencil skirt.

Several times she'd slid her fingers around them, desperately tempted to give him a call. Then the past would flood in, crawling around her senses with painful reminders of what had happened the last time she'd tried to reach him.

'Are you feeling all right, Cassie?' Ella came to stand beside her desk. 'You look dreadfully pale.'

Her shadow honed his sharp eyes on her. Fresh tension fizzed across her skin. 'I'm fine,' she responded, 'just—'

'Feeling hunted,' Ella put in, flicking a knife-edged glance at the shadow, who quickly lowered his gaze. 'Come on, let's take an early lunch,' she insisted. 'You look like you could do with some fresh air and a break.'

They bought sandwiches and coffee from the local sandwich bar and walked across the road to the small gated park set in the middle of the square on which the BarTec building was situated. Finding a vacant bench beneath a tree, they sat down. It was quite warm for October and the sun glinted down through the tree branches still heavy with autumn-gold leaves.

'OK,' Ella said, flipping the lid off her coffee, 'let me tell you what I know, then you can fill in the empty spaces… Our sexy new boss is the twins' father. Don't bother to deny it because I worked that one out straight away,' she warned when Cassie opened her mouth to speak. 'I don't think Pandora Batiste has worked out that part yet but she certainly feels threatened by you, which is why she spent last week on your case.'

Cassie laughed bleakly. 'Wouldn't you feel threatened if he was your lover?'

'Maybe,' Ella conceded. 'More than maybe, if she knows that you and the twins spent Saturday with him—and don't deny that one either because I was coming to see you when I saw you return in his car. That sweet little scene on the pavement outside your apartment made me change my mind and leave you all to it.'

'You should have hung around longer, then,' Cassie murmured dryly. 'You would have been able to watch him depart.'

'For good?' Ella questioned sharply.

Cassie shrugged. 'Who knows?'

'Is that why you've looked so done-in and pale this week?'

This time Cassie's shrug arrived without an added comment.

'Idiot.' Ella sighed. 'Want to tell me how the two of you came together in the first place?' she encouraged. 'Six years ago you must have been a real babe-in-arms to a man like him.'

'He's only five years older than me, Ella! You can't label him a cradle-snatcher.'

'Just a rake on the take?'

'No!' She sighed out, frowning because wasn't that exactly how she'd come to think of Sandro until he turned up again and told her about his accident and his lost memory? 'Can we stop this now? I'm hungry; I want to eat my sandwich!'

'I'm not stopping you eating,' Ella denied. 'You're doing that to yourself because you're in waste-away mode.'

Waste-away mode probably described her perfectly, Cassie acknowledged heavily—or lost in a limbo caused by Sandro's continuing silence. Perhaps he was intending to just turn up at BarTec on Friday morning and haul her off to be married before he delivered her back to her desk. Or perhaps he'd done another U-turn and changed his mind about the whole crazy—

'Perhaps you will cheer up when I tell you that Pandora Batiste hasn't shown her face because she's been sent back to Florence at the boss's command,' Ella said coolly.

So that was why she hadn't seen the other woman. And she didn't feel any better about the news because…what was Florence except for another city for two lovers to meet up in?

Shifting restlessly where she sat, Cassie almost knocked over her Styrofoam coffee cup where she'd placed it beside her on the bench. Catching it before it spilt, she set it straight again then dropped her untouched sandwich beside it with a sigh.

A squirrel scurried past them with its mouth stuffed with acorns. Cassie watched it disappear into a mound of fallen leaves at the base of a tree. It was busy, focused, absolutely certain about what it was doing and why it was doing it and she envied it that because she wasn't sure about anything.

Why hadn't he called as he'd promised? Was he with Pandora in Florence? Would he do that to her? Her head told her no. Her *head* told her that he possessed a perfectly acceptable and for-givable reason for what he'd done six years ago, but her emotions still clung to the hurt he'd inflicted on them when he'd told her to get lost in that phone call she'd made to him, and a need to maintain her defences so he couldn't hurt her like that again.

She didn't know him, not really, and he certainly didn't know her. They were like two strangers linked by an act of fate that had given them equal shares in two children conceived during a single night of fabulous sex. Was that enough to warrant marriage between them? Wouldn't it be more sensible to arrange joint custody with equal shares in the twins' upbringing? Had she even agreed that she would marry him at all?

No, she hadn't, and Sandro had no darn right to assume that she had done, or to leave her hanging in limbo like this.

'And here's the really interesting bit,' Ella continued, sipping at her Styrofoam cup. 'Just before I hauled you out here to grill you, I received a call from Gio, instructing me to clear your diary of all your appointments and to pass them to your shadow. Apparently the boss is—'

'Standing right in front of you,' Sandro's own smooth, fabulously accented voice cut in.

Both heads shot up in unison, Ella choking back the words she had been about to speak, Cassie gripped by a shockingly violent surge of relief.

He looked so tall and lean and sense-stirringly vital, the dappling sunlight seeping down through the trees just loving his healthy, warm golden tan. His dark eyes glinted as he looked down at her through the framework formed by his luxurious eyelashes, which made the look frankly as sexy as hell. But his mouth wore a grim look of disapproval that made her suddenly stingingly aware of her old grey suit she'd flung on without much thought this morning, and the way she'd carelessly scraped back her hair. She even clenched her fingers to stop them from lifting up to check how untidy her hair actually was.

Whereas Sandro's hair was fabulously groomed to suit his elegant features; same with the dark silk suit he was wearing that looked as though this was the first time it had ever seen the light of day. His shirt was white with a fine red stripe running through it, his slender silk tie a darker red colour that drew her unwilling gaze down its length until she met with the narrow bowl of his hips. And the power hinted at in his long, dark-suited legs should be censored, she decided as her mouth ran dry and she had to drag her eyes away from him, restless fingers clenching even tighter because she wanted to rip the elegant suit of clothes right off him so she could look at the man.

The physically potent and sexual man.

She wanted him. It was that quick, that hot and violent. She wanted him naked and flat on his back somewhere. She wanted to check him all over with her eyes and her hands and her mouth.

'Where have you been?' The question shot from her more sharply than she intended.

Sandro wondered what she would say if he told her he'd spent the last three days closeted in his apartment with his brother, enduring a living kind of hell. It did not help his stinging conscience to know that his three days of hell had finally given him back his memory. Learning the truth—knowing the full truth at last about what had really taken place six years ago—did not alter the miserable fact that this woman he was looking at here, with her pale complexion and her dark green defensive eyes and her fragile, tense posture, had paid the full price for his own bloody sins.

'Enjoying my last few days of freedom,' he replied to her question with a grim satire that he knew would fly right over her head.

In Florence with Pandora? Cassie wondered. 'Well, I hope it was worth it.'

'Very much so,' he assured—then he struck with the lightning speed of a jungle cat, bending to take hold of her by her shoulders and draw her to her feet.

Next thing Cassie knew she was plastered against him; a second after that and she was on the receiving end of a hot, very possessive and hungry kiss. Just like that, and out here in broad daylight with Ella looking on avidly, he explored her mouth with the determined intimacy of a man staking claim on what he perceived to be already his.

And Cassie didn't just let him, she encouraged him, arching into his long length, letting her fingers trail up his jacket to his shoulders then further until they'd buried themselves in the silky black hair at his nape.

By the time he released her mouth she was weak and dizzy, her breathing a thick, gasping sound of complaint.

'You missed me,' he said with fierce satisfaction, sending a surge of heat pouring into her cheeks.

'I was worried, that's all. You said you would call me.'

'Well, I'm fine and I'm here.' He claimed her mouth for a second brief burn of possession. 'Enjoy the rest of your lunch,' he said to Ella then, and without so much as offering the other girl a glance he banded an arm across Cassie's back and turned them around and walked them away.

'That was just so rude!' Cassie gasped out in protest.

'Your friend has witnessed enough from us to make her flavour of the month at BarTec,' Sandro countered arrogantly.

'Ella isn't a gossip.'

'Then you can make it up to her by inviting her to our wedding.'

'I haven't said that I will marry you!'

'But you will.'

He fed her into his waiting car before she could answer, forcing her to slither quickly across the seat again as he followed her inside. When she turned to face him, ready with a stinging objection to his cool assurance, Sandro was ready for it.

'You prefer to hurt and disappoint our children?' he challenged, settling his long frame into the plush leather seat.

'I have a right to consider my own feelings too!'

'Then perhaps you prefer me to use more ruthless methods to convince you,' he offered, using those ink-dark eyes to convey his meaning to her.

He was talking about sex, reminding her of the clinch they'd just shared in the park and her own lack of control. Cassie's lips parted and trembled revealingly. Heat drenched her bones. She could fight him any which way there was to fight him—except when he touched her. She hated the fact that Sandro knew it. This physical hold he had over her laid waste to the six years she'd spent rebuilding her respect for herself.

Sandro didn't remember her but, like any good-looking, sexually active male, he could pick out an easy target and go for it—because it was there to take. The difference with her was that he was prepared to offer marriage because of this turn of fate that linked them via the twins.

Without them she would be just another notch on his bedpost, another conquest to love and leave. And no amount of justification due to his lost memory was ever going to rid her of the gut feeling that even without the car crash he would have left her anyway.

I don't know you. I don't want to know you. Please don't call this number again.

A shiver ran down the length of her taut backbone. Cassie wrenched her eyes away from him, wishing badly she could wipe those words from her memory, then maybe she wouldn't feel so at war with herself, as well as with him.

Had he spent the last few days with Pandora?

Did she really want to know?

The car moved off with the smoothness of a thoroughbred. As they drove in front of the BarTec building, she remembered what Ella had told her just before Sandro had arrived to interrupt.

'You've terminated my employment, haven't you?' The question left her husky and taut.

'What makes you think that?'

Turning to look at him, she saw genuine curiosity glinting in his eyes and he even portrayed that sexily. Definitely at war with herself now,

Cassie relayed what Ella had said about her shadow taking over her duties.

'So you've decided I did this to pile the pressure on you?'

'Well, didn't you?'

He frowned with impatience. 'You cannot commute to London from Florence, *cara*, and a more trusting woman would have worked that out for herself. But in answer to your accusation…no, I have not terminated your employment. You are merely on a few months' leave in which to get married and resettle in another country. When you are ready—*if* you decide you want to continue to work—then we will find you a position in one of my organisations that work out of Florence.' He waved a long-fingered hand. 'It is a decision I will leave to you.'

Not even slightly mollified by that perfectly reasonable speech, 'Gosh, my one small concession in a battery of your pre-decided edicts. Thank you!' she said.

'It was not a concession,' he denied. 'If you knew me better you would know I don't make them…I actually believe you have a right of choice whether or not you want to continue to work after we marry.'

'*If* I marry you.' Cassie still couldn't seem to stop hedging on that subject. It was as if some itchy instinct was obstinately stopping her from giving in to him. 'And you can say what you like, Sandro, but the truth is that you want me cornered, isolated and helpless so I'll stop arguing with you.'

He heaved out a heavy sigh. 'If I was being that ruthless then it didn't work! Believe it or not, I thought that we had the marriage issue tied up!'

'If you believed that then why didn't you call me to warn me that my shadow was there to learn my job?'

'Because…' He stopped, his lips coming together with a grim, hard snap. He frowned and looked away from her, only to immediately look back again, frustration playing games with the set of his face. 'I was busy, OK?' he said finally. 'I had…things to do that put me out of range of a satellite link. And will you please desist from perching on the edge of the seat emulating a stern school headmistress?' he bit out suddenly, waving a long-fingered hand at her tense attitude. Then he really shocked her with a sudden, totally unexpected eruption of anger. 'And fasten your damn seatbelt!'

She was startled enough to jerk in surprise, the lightning-quick way he snaked across the gap between them and physically pressed her back into the seat stunning Cassie into uttering a sharp cry.

'You fool,' he muttered, dragging the seatbelt around her and pushing it firmly into its lock. 'Trust me, *cara*, you do not want to know what it feels like to hit something at speed without this in place!'

Flung by the taut words and his roughened manner into visualising what it was he was talking about, 'I'm sorry,' she mumbled. 'I just didn't think.'

'Been there, done that.' His mouth wore a ring of tension around it. As he went to move away from her, Cassie reached up to touch his cheek. He looked at her, glinting eyes still frowning and fierce.

'Sorry,' she repeated.

His answering sigh turned into a grimace. 'I overreacted, didn't I?'

'No,' she denied. 'I deserved to be physically

manhandled and shocked out of my skin.' Her fingertips stroked the tension etched into his lean cheekbone. 'We haven't really discussed what happened to you in the accident but—'

'We are not going to discuss it.'

As abruptly as he'd moved across the seat he shifted back again, the subject cut off as severely as he severed Cassie's breath in her throat. Her eyelashes flickered as she studied his lean profile. He looked stern suddenly.

'Sandro—'

'I was going to take you to lunch, but I've changed my mind,' he cut right over her. 'We will go shopping instead.'

'Shopping for what?' she demanded blankly.

'Wedding rings. Betrothal rings. A bridal gown that will knock my eyes out,' he enlightened casually. 'Perhaps a treat or two for the twins.'

Being met by a wall of silence in response to that, Sandro was forced to turn his head. His beautiful bride was sitting there in her neat grey business suit with her long legs crossed decorously in front of her and her face showing him a stubborn profile that completely wiped out the few moments of softness which had preceded it.

The air left his lungs on an impatient hiss. Every time he showed her vulnerability she showed him softness. Every time he tried to move things forward for them she showed him stubborn ice.

'Stop fighting me,' he advised. 'I understand why you feel the need to do it but I won't let it change the final outcome. We get married in two days. Accept it, Cassie.'

She turned to look at him, green eyes Arctic-cool, her soft mouth small. 'Most decent men would have the grace to *ask* me to marry them.'

Wry acknowledgement stretched his mouth to a grin—then suddenly he wasn't grinning as a vivid flashback completely caught him out. Sandro thought he'd done with them during his three days of hell, but this flashback was different from the rest he'd experienced and sent a blanket of heat flooding through his body as he captured an image of her lying naked on a narrow bed with her long, slender body backed by a pale pink coverlet and her hair fanned out around her face. Those cool green eyes were shy and dark and luminous, that stubborn mouth softly parted, red and ripe.

Marry me, Cassie...

'*Dio,*' he breathed at the husky, dark echo of his own deep voice, and slammed his eyes shut as her soft response ignited a blazing fire in his loins with a force that actually made him shake.

'*Tomorrow,*' she'd whispered.

'Sandro...?' The sound of her voice saying his name cut into the flow of this new memory. He felt her hand curve around his arm.

'Sandro,' she repeated anxiously, 'don't.'

Like a man flung from one place to another he came back to a sense of the present with his full attention focusing on her trembling fingers clutching his arm through his suit jacket. She thought he was about to black out again but nothing could be further from the truth. What he'd just experienced had arrived with crystal clarity backed up by a three-day war he'd been waging with his past.

The one that got away, he thought ruefully as he fought to control the heat of his raging hormones. Lifting his gaze to her face, he found he was drowning in dark green anxiety. He loved it. He loved the way her teeth were worrying her full, soft lower lip.

'I'm OK,' he said, but she wasn't having it.

'No, you're not.' Straining the seatbelt to reach out with her other hand, she laid it against the rapid beat of his heart. 'What triggered it this time?'

From aggravatingly stubborn to gloriously concerned, Sandro observed, relaxing like a stroked cat into the seat, ruthlessly ready to pump this moment for all that it was worth.

'You did—who else?' he responded truthfully, then confided, 'I saw you lying gloriously naked on a very girly pink bed.'

Hot colour poured into her cheeks and he had to fight the urge to laugh. She understood what it was he was referring to. She knew exactly what he'd seen.

'It was very—intense.' Reaching up, he lifted her hand away from his chest and raised it to his lips. 'Sexy,' he added, laying kisses along the tops of her fingers, 'disgracefully passionate.'

'I… You…' Her slender body tensed like a bow string.

Sandro let his eyes take on a darkling glint. 'I was telling you I loved you—'

'You don't have to describe it,' Cassie cut in. 'I'm not the one with the patchy memory!'

'And you whispered back to me, *"I love you too, Sandro..."*'

Cassie hid her eyes beneath her trembling eye-lashes and tried to pull away from him but Sandro tightened his grip.

'Did you mean it, *mi amore*?' he persisted softly. 'Did *I* mean it?'

At the time...? 'Yes,' she breathed.

'Then we can mean it again. All it needs is a leap of faith.'

He was talking marriage again. He hadn't really stopped talking marriage! Only now he was calling it a leap of faith. Unclipping her fingers from his hard-muscled bicep, she tried once again to retreat.

'I asked you to marry me—'

She swung on him hotly. 'Will you stop telling me what I already know?'

She'd been there, after all! She didn't have a single problem recalling every detail of their first time together in her tiny apartment in her even tinier bedroom with its narrow, girly pink bed!

'So I'm asking you again—will you marry me?'

He was remorseless, that was what he was—

pig remorseless! Shame he couldn't remember the way he'd kissed her goodbye the morning after and walked away!

'If I am willing to take the leap then why can't you take it with me…?'

Cassie opened her eyes to stare at him. There was no hint of strain blanching out his lean golden features, no sign at all of that terrible weakness that usually befell him after a memory flash like this. He was simply Sandro, lean, dark, beautiful Sandro, with the disgustingly long, curling black eyelashes framing dark, dark sexy brown eyes and the warm, smooth, achingly sensual mouth she just wanted to…

'OK!' she snapped out in resentful surrender. 'I'll marry you! But don't think for one second that your lousy lost memory means I forgive you for what you did to me because it doesn't!' She rose up on the back of that surrender. 'And nor will I forgive you for the unscrupulous way you dragged the twins into this!'

His response was immediate and downright arrogant. With a fast, graceful movement of his long body he had her imprisoned in her own corner of the seat. Her quivering gasp of surprise found a vent in a stinging, 'You've unfastened your seatbelt!'

'The car is stopped; now I can do what I want with you.'

And he did. It was no use pretending she didn't let him when she didn't put up even a token fight to the hot, consuming demand of his kiss. She came out of it breathless and disheveled, her jacket spread open, her blouse buttons undone and the twin peaks of her breasts stinging against the flimsy lace bra cups because they wanted his caressing fingers back on them. Her hair flowed around her shoulders now, though she couldn't recall him setting it free, and her mouth tingled hot and bruised and swollen.

'There…' with husky satisfaction he ran the tip of his tongue along her pulsing upper lip '…leap of faith, sealed with a kiss. Now let's go shopping….'

CHAPTER NINE

CLIMBING out of the car to find the driver had parked in the middle of Bond Street put a deeper blush into Cassie's already hot cheeks. For a moment she froze, agonisingly aware that she'd barely been given time to do up enough blouse buttons before Sandro had caught hold of her hand and pulled her out onto the street.

And they'd stopped outside one of the most famous jewellers in London. Staring at its elegant glass frontage, she saw none of the glistening riches set out on display because she was staring at her own reflection in shocked dismay.

She looked like a lush again, a tousle-haired, deep-cleavaged blonde lush with a thoroughly kissed mouth and dazed, dark, river-green eyes. It took only a glance at Sandro's expression to know that he was very happy with what he saw as he looked back at her. And he looked no different from the way he had when he'd first appeared in front of her in the park. His clothes were still immaculate, his hair smooth and neat. Yet she knew, because she'd watched him do it, that he'd had to adjust certain parts of his anatomy before he'd opened the car door.

And recalling why he'd had to do that did not ease the heat from her cheeks as he walked her across the pavement, or what was still taking place between her trembling thighs.

'I really do hate you,' she whispered as they waited for a liveried security person to swing the jeweller's shop door open for them.

'I know…' he bent his dark head to touch his warm lips to her ear '…fabulous hatred, *amante mia*. I can't wait to enjoy it some more.'

With that rich promise ringing in her head, he walked them into the shop, her hand secured inside his. The way he received instant gushing attention kept her quiet and meek because— well, there was only room for one ego in the shop and to watch Sandro turn his arrogant Italian ego full on was something she discovered she would not have liked to miss.

They were escorted to a private room from

where he plied her with diamonds and rubies and sapphires. He waved away the emeralds with long-fingered contempt because, 'They cannot compete with your beautiful eyes, *bella mia*,' he told her. When she lifted those beautiful emerald eyes to stare at him as if he'd turned into some weird caricature of himself, his lazy grin told her he knew exactly how he was behaving and was enjoying doing it.

He was different all round, Cassie realised, light-hearted, more expressive, expansive in his language and his warm, sensual drawl. He draped her in diamonds, necklaces, bracelets, and made her cheeks burn like fire when he used the tips of his long fingers to delicately position a huge white diamond droplet between the thrusting warmth of her breasts.

'Will you stop it?' she hissed at him when the assistant moved off to collect another tray of mind-boggling trinkets. 'I'm not going to let you buy me any of them. And I feel like a bimbo!'

'I'm buying you this one,' he said, leaning against the table while she stood in front of him. 'I'm going to eat it on our wedding night as a sexy side dish while I am eating you.'

'You're mad,' she breathed helplessly.

'Crazy,' he agreed. He didn't need to extend that to 'crazy for you' because it was written in his eyes as he caught up the diamond droplet and lifted it to his lips before settling it between her breasts again.

Cassie knew she had started to fall fathoms deep in love with him again when it occurred to her that this madly extravagant display he was putting on was not about playing games or about his ego or even the shockingly sexual atmosphere he was generating deliberately.

He was, quite simply, being the other Sandro she'd met years ago. The relaxed, light-hearted, teasing, charming, gorgeously expressive Sandro she'd spent two amazing weeks falling deeper in love with every day. This was Sandro being happy. It hit her really hard just how *un*happy he had been since they'd met up again—and the reason for the change…?

She'd stopped fighting him. She'd given him what he wanted and agreed to marry him. She didn't think this was even about the twins. He might not remember her but, as he kept on saying to her, he *knew* her. He'd slipped back into wanting her from almost the first moment their eyes had met again, and now he was courting her—because this crazy romantic side to his nature came so beautifully naturally to him.

That had to mean something, didn't it? It had to mean that his instincts were not playing him false and if—*when*—his memory did return it was not going to reveal some terrible, dark reason as to why he'd shut her out in the first place.

They chose a diamond cluster ring that sparkled on her finger. And matching wedding rings studded with tiny bright diamonds set into rich yellow gold.

From there he changed his mind again and decided to take her to lunch at a busy pub, where they had to stand up at a bar table to eat and the lunch crowd pressed in all around them but they didn't notice because they were talking—really talking the way they had used to do, about everything and anything.

Engrossed.

Touching, always touching each other without really being aware of doing it, his fingers toying with her fingers, stroking her cheek, the tumbling waterfall of her hair. Her fingers feeding him crisp slices of green apple from her dessert dish he bit into with his even white teeth, always making sure he grazed her tingling fingertips at the same time. Other women stared covetously at him and enviously at her. And the sexual magnetism purred around the two of them like the idling engine of a dangerously powerful car.

It was as if he was recreating their first afternoon together without being aware of it. And Cassie sank beneath his magical spell. As they walked back down Bond Street with his arm resting about her shoulders she expected them to start shopping as he'd said they would, but he shrugged that idea away with, 'We'll do it tomorrow.'

Tomorrow suddenly felt bright and exciting because it had to mean he intended to spend it with her.

Cracks only began to appear in the veneer of their reincarnation when he came back with her to her apartment and saw how they lived for the first time.

He didn't say a single word as he looked at the stuffed old armchair and twin-seater sofa made to match by the couple of throws draped over them. Then he took in the ancient TV set with its tiny square screen. When he finally dealt his gaze on the wooden dining furniture bought flat-packed on her shoestring budget and put together by her own hands, it was as if a suit of glass armour shot down over him. He might as well have bitten out, My children live in a place like this…?

'Don't be such a snob, Sandro,' Cassie retaliated stiffly. 'We have been very happy here.'

Walking out of the room, she crossed the tiny hallway to gain access to her bedroom. Flushed and cross and her dignity ruffled, she opened her wardrobe door and slipped her jacket onto a hanger.

A sound behind her made her turn as she closed the wardrobe door. He was standing in the doorway, giving her tiny bedroom with its single bed and single wardrobe and single chest of drawers that same glassy look.

'If you're looking for pink, try the other bedroom,' she said in an attempt to lighten the loaded atmosphere.

He didn't even crack half a smile. What he did do was to take the single step to reach her wardrobe and draw the door open then stood staring at what was hanging inside it—the little black dress she'd worn to his introduction dinner, freshly dry-cleaned now and covered in polythene, another suit like the one she'd been wearing today and a small selection of business-like tops and shirts.

Grim mouth flattening, he slammed the door shut then spun on his heel and walked out. When she'd fought her angry flush enough to follow him she found him standing in the twins' room as if he'd been turned to stone. One side of the room was as pink and feminine as a fairy tale, the other side shot with moons and rockets and flying space troopers.

'What did you expect?' she flung out, hurt by his oh-so-expressive stance. 'A damn huge, great, fancy palace?'

The fact that she swore at him swung Sandro around. Cassie was stunned that the pallor was back on his face—only this time it was the harsh pallor of contempt.

'This is our *home*!' she pressed on him angrily. 'Don't you dare turn your rich nose up at it!'

'I wasn't—'

'You were,' she said on a shimmer of burning offence. 'But don't worry, Sandro. Bella is looking forward to the day her handsome daddy prince carries us all off to his fabulous castle! So if you don't have a castle, take my advice and *buy* one! She will love you to bits for making all her fairy-tale dreams come true! Anthony might not, but then he's more concerned about communicating when he can't speak Italian. And I don't think for one minute that he's nurturing dreams of you producing your own private rocket to the stars!'

She spun away, her wild, bubbling fever of offended dignity spoiled by the hot burn of hurt tears.

'I already own the castle.'

Cassie froze in the doorway, narrow shoulders racking back, quivering and taut inside her white blouse.

'And my own jet.' His voice sounded jerky and thick. 'I own several more residences in far-flung, exotic places, a couple of helicopters, an ocean-going yacht and an island in the Caribbean,' he listed, almost—almost sounding apologetic to Cassie's oversensitive ears. 'What

I don't have is what you have right here, which is a *home*, as you said. Warmth, untidy comfort.' His impatient sigh had her turning about. 'Now I'm going to have to rethink my whole approach to what it was I thought would impress you and the twins when we hit Florence…' His mouth flattened out even further. 'You must have hated my London apartment.'

'It reminded me of a big, echoing mausoleum,' Cassie murmured, coming down from hurt dignity but still hanging on to the threat of tears. 'I'm…sorry if I misunderstood your reaction but—'

'But now you're in trouble,' Sandro said for her.

Her own finish for that sentence was swallowed down when she looked into his glowing dark eyes and saw what he was talking about. He reached out to take hold of her shoulders, the small gap between them suddenly shut. A pulse beat accelerated in her throat, a short gasp escaping when her breasts stung as they filled with heat.

'You've been warned before about feeling sorry for me.' Sliding his hands down the length of her body, he closed them on her hips and tugged.

Shock widened Cassie's eyes. 'Y-you…'

'*Sí,*' he confirmed, making her feel the full, probing state of his arousal. 'Liquid green eyes and sympathy…control-killers,' he stated darkly.

A vivid image of burning gas jets flew across her mind and brought the pink tip of her tongue snaking out to touch the tingling curve of her upper lip. A lusty growl and he caught that pink tip between his lips and sucked. He was already backing her out of the twins' bedroom, the shockingly rampant evidence of his intentions building in strength with the stimulation of the move. Her hands had to clutch at his arms to maintain her balance because he was really kissing her now, exploring her mouth with a sensual expertise and urgency that arched her neck, and pressed her breasts into firmer contact with his chest.

She could feel the heavy pump of his heart, his heat, the sheer masculine dominance of his hard male contours turning her female softness to a quivering, sensual flow of warm blood. When she heard the sound of a door shutting and instantly recognised it as her own bedroom door, she had to fight to drag her mouth from his.

'We can't,' she groaned.

'We can,' he insisted, then added with a searing rasp of amusement, 'We must,' and buried his mouth in the heated hollow of her throat.

'But school—the twins!' she tried again—desperately.

At least she succeeded in bringing his dark head up. His eyes looked like black pits filled with flaming frustration, his lips were parted, warm and soft.

'How long?' he demanded, tension holding him like a string of prickling barbed wire.

Cassie tried to think without taking her wary eyes off him to look at her bedside clock. She didn't trust him. She could still feel the powering urgency being pressed against her, and her own body wasn't behaving itself. There was a pulsing ache taking place deep down in her abdomen, sensual moisture already livening the tender place between her thighs.

She tried for a breath. He was waiting for an answer, taut and bold and still. Her head twisted round, eyelashes flickering as she glanced away from him at the clock then back to him again.

'H-half an hour.' She watched his frustration

flare to monumental proportions and like a rat throwing itself on a trap she sealed her own immediate destiny. 'Jenny, m-my neighbour, picks them up, s-so let's call it forty-f-five minutes before they get back...'

The flare of frustration became a glow of pure arrogance. 'I can work within those parameters,' he drawled.

Next second her pencil skirt dropped to the floor. The veins in her slender thighs started to sting as her blood began to race through them. Sandro was yanking his tie off, eyes fixed and intent on her face. He stripped with a grace and a speed that held her breathless and speechless.

'If you want the truth, I wasn't going to do this,' he admitted, the lithe move of his hips seeing his trousers stripped from his legs along with whatever else he was wearing beneath.

'Do what?' Cassie couldn't stop staring. He was magnificent naked.

'Make love to you again before we married.' He fed his arms around her and drew her against all of that taut masculinity, uncaring, so assured about the perfection of his own body. 'I was going to make us wait, build on the tension so you'd be so hot for me you wouldn't think of changing your mind.'

'Arrogant,' Cassie shook out as he slipped her blouse from her body and unclipped her bra.

He didn't even complain that she'd been too shy to strip herself. He caught the weight of her breasts in his palms and lifted them to meet with his lowering mouth. The sharp sting of pleasure that shot through her body forced a shaken gasp from her throat.

On a low growl he caught it, licked it from her lips as it arrived there. His hands followed the smooth, squirming contours of her body right down to her bottom, which he cupped, then lifted her into the waiting bowl of his pelvis and the tasting kiss jumped into pure, naked heat. He just took and kept control of her senses through the energy in his body and the direction of his kisses, stripping her of the final layers of her clothing until finally—gratefully, he laid her down beneath him on her narrow bed.

No more talk—no breath spare for it. The fever took over from the moment he lay down beside her then rolled towards her and sent his long fingers stroking into the warm, moist juncture of her thighs. He roughed out a string of soft curses when he discovered she was so ready for him.

Weak, fretful, clinging to him, green eyes washed with pleading as they clung to his smouldering dark glare, he caressed her into a writhing turmoil of agitated pleasure, watching—watching as she fell apart for him. It did not occur to her that giving her pleasure heightened his own until she reached down to clasp him and watched him fall apart too. His control fled on the single ragged breath he took, and he ran his eyes over her with a fierce possessiveness that verged on the wild. Her whimper of protest when he drew back from what he was doing for her was replaced by a series of fevered groans in answer to the exquisite caresses he plied across her quivering flesh. By the time the first driving thrust into her came she lost what bit of sanity she had left.

'Cassie…' he breathed into her mouth as the intensity of what she was experiencing caught hold of him too.

Her fingernails clawed twin death grips into his shoulder muscles, her lungs fighting for breath against the hot urgency of his mouth. She was aware she was losing touch with reality, aware that he was losing it with her, aware that they climbed the towering walls of excitement together and even let go together, tumbling into the long, rolling waves of intense, soul-shuddering release.

Last time they'd done this it had been wild and uncontrolled. This time it crossed both those barriers to reach a different level entirely. Coming down from it was physically painful; letting her grip on it slip away was like giving up an elemental part of herself. She couldn't move, couldn't speak, couldn't make her limbs work, so they remained wrapped around his hot, sweat-slicked, muscle-flexed frame.

He touched his lips to her hot cheek and she felt his tremor. His fingers were unsteady as he used them to comb her tumbled hair back from her face. When she managed to lift up her heavy eyelids she saw his eyes were too black to be real, glazed and drunk on what they'd shared. They didn't speak; their eyes did it for them. No smiles, no teasing, no attempt at a joke to ease them from this point on to what had to follow—the final touchdown with earth again, the separation.

As her legs finally allowed her to relax their hold on him, they slid down his powerful thighs and legs without breaking contact with his warm golden skin. He was heavy on her but she liked it, liked the way her breasts were crushed against his hair-roughened chest and the flat of her stomach took the weight of his pelvis. He strung slow, gentle kisses along the satin arch of her eyebrows, the top of her nose, then her mouth again, and the tension in her arms slowly relaxed, her fingers feathering across his wide, muscled shoulders then the line of his jaw and onto his cheeks.

This was how it had been for them their first time together—every time they'd come together during that long, fruitful night in her narrow, girly pink bed.

How could he have forgotten that? How could he have wiped it from his memory as if it had been nothing worth remembering?

The doorbell gave a sharp, stinging peal, screaming through her head like an alarm bell and dumping her rudely back into now.

'Oh, my God, the twins,' she gasped, launching him off her with the strength of ten women and jackknifing to her feet.

Her legs were still luxuriating in a million warm tingles, so making them move was the most difficult process. Grabbing up her robe because it was the nearest thing to her, Cassie dragged it on over her love-flushed body. Forty-five minutes…they'd been lost in what they'd been doing for forty-five minutes! It sent her dizzy just thinking about it.

'For goodness' sake, move, Sandro!' she shook out at him because he was still lying on her narrow bed how she'd left him, flat on his back with the long length of his nakedness on full display.

Cassie reeled her gaze away from him and opened the bedroom door, her fingers trembling as they tried to comb her hair out of its disarray as she reached for the front door latch and opened it to face her two children and her next-door neighbour feeling what could only be described as as guilty as her wildly flushing skin.

'Our daddy is here!' Bella squealed in excitement.

'We saw his car outside!' Anthony joined in.

Jenny said nothing; however, her wide-eyed expression had plenty to say, which had Cassie clutching her robe to her throat. 'S-sorry,' was all she could find to offer to the other woman. 'I should have called you to—'

A sound directly behind her sent her head swivelling round as the twins barged past her with excited shrieks, totally uncaring that their mother was dressed in her bathrobe, only caring about one thing: reaching Sandro, who had come out of the bedroom, when Cassie would have much preferred him to remain hidden away in there. Now he was filling the tiny hallway with his lean, dark presence as he greeted the children with light touches to their heads and smiles.

She didn't know how he'd done it in the time available but he'd pulled on his shirt, trousers and shoes—no socks, she noticed with an inconsequence which almost made her burst forth with a hysterical laugh. His dark hair was mussed, eyes still heavy with what they'd been doing, the cuffs of his shirt hanging loose around his wrists. He might as well have stepped out here naked, she thought helplessly, cheeks burning all the more. When he caught her expression he raised a wickedly satirical eyebrow then stepped up and drew her back against him with an arm he looped around her waist.

The twins were talking ten to the dozen to him. Bella had a grip on his other hand while Anthony became tangled up in his feet. Ignoring her tension, he looked at the older woman over the top of Cassie's tumbled blonde head and said, 'Ah, the only person in the world to whom my future wife will entrust the care of our children. It is a great pleasure to meet you at last, Mrs Dean…'

Charm oozed from every beautifully accented syllable. Jenny wasn't immune to it. By the time they closed the door, the short and portly fizzy grey-haired lady who'd been happily married for forty-five years had been totally and incurably seduced into adoring a man equipped to turn any woman's head when he set his mind to it.

'That was horrible,' Cassie breathed as she wilted against the wall behind her, her whole body still wearing a heated blush.

'I assume by your reaction that your neighbour isn't used to catching you out like this,' Sandro said dryly.

If he'd meant it as a joke, Cassie wasn't laughing. With no gap in between she turned from hot to ice. He was implying that she brought other men here for a quick roll on her bed—or was he asking her if she did?

Whichever; aware of the twins' presence or she would be tearing angry holes into him, 'Excuse me,' she murmured frigidly, and with a twist of her body she disappeared to the other side of her bedroom door before he could say anything else.

How dared he make such an insulting assumption—how dared he believe he even had the right to comment on her love life?

Her bed still wore the imprint of their bodies. On a flare of skin-flaying anger she stepped over to it and yanked the duvet straight with more violence than the task warranted. The floor was littered with their discarded clothing. It reminded her of the bedroom in his apartment as she started scooping them up. Perhaps these fevered losses of control were all they were fit for, she posed bitterly as she tossed the clothes down onto the bed.

Had he dared to say that because it was how he ran his own life? Was *he* so used to being caught out with his pants down that he could be so casual about it? Her breath seethed out from between her tense teeth as she stripped her robe off. Beyond the closed bedroom door she could hear the twins talking excitedly to him and his deep-timbred responses.

How was she supposed to have carried on a sex life with two children always around? she felt like opening the door to toss at him! He was the one who'd maintained his sexual freedom for the last six years! She was the one who'd had it thoroughly curbed before it had barely begun!

And he still hadn't answered the question about his relationship with Pandora Batiste. For all she knew he'd been bedding the dark-haired beauty throughout his disappearance this week!

Dragging on a pair of jeans and a long-sleeved skinny top, she spent a few minutes putting her clothes away then picked up Sandro's remaining clothes and took them with her out of the bedroom and into the living room, where the sight which met her eyes stopped her dead.

Sandro was sitting on the floor with his back against the sofa, long legs stretched out beneath the coffee table. Bella was on his lap—curled there wearing a rapt expression Cassie had never seen on her daughter's face before and it hurt something tender inside her to see it there now. Anthony was standing by Sandro's right shoulder, gravely instructing him how to fashion an aeroplane out of a piece of brightly coloured A4 paper. The room already wore the evidence of several failed attempts, though she doubted that someone with Sandro's agile capabilities needed so many tries to get the simple construction right.

And Sandro himself held his daughter safe within the curve of an arm while his dark gaze was fixed intently on his son. Tears stung the backs of Cassie's eyelids because she could see the wonder in his expression as he listened to Anthony, feel the edge of his vulnerability in the arm he had looped around Bella. All three were bonding in their own unique fashion, Bella with her innate tactile nature by cuddling, Anthony with the serious practicality of his technical skills, Sandro by accommodating both twins' needs, at the same time bonding them together as a heart-wrenchingly tight trio.

For the first time in the twins' five-year existence Cassie learnt what it felt like to be a separate part of them, and it hurt. She saw what the twins had been missing having no contact with their father. She saw what Sandro had missed out on by not knowing them.

The reason why she had Sandro's clothes draped over her arm felt suddenly petty. What had she been intending to do with them—toss them at him before she threw him out on an act of angry bitterness that would have severed that fragile bond she was witnessing here?

She turned away from the living room unde- tected, and went to place the clothes back on the bed before slipping quietly into her tiny kitchen, where she stood, staring out of the window with no idea what she was thinking, or what she was feeling, only aware that something inside her had changed.

The emphasis on what was important had changed, she realised after a few minutes. For the last ten mad days she'd been totally focused on her own emotions—anger, resentment, sus- picion, betrayal, the heated passion that kept flaring up between her and Sandro, usually followed by fresh confrontation because ev- erything inside her was so mixed up and defen- sive and at war. The twins' wants and needs had become swallowed up by it all; now they rose to the surface and swamped everything else beneath a shivery wave. *They* needed a father whether or not she needed a husband. They needed Sandro even though she knew she was still fighting demons about him.

'What's wrong?'

His quiet voice came from the kitchen doorway. Turning her head, she saw him standing there with his hands thrust into his trouser pockets and his shirt still open at its collar and cuffs. He looked sombre, wary, as if he'd picked her mood up from the other room and forced himself to come in here.

'Where are the twins?' she questioned quietly.

'Watching television.' His eyelids were half covering his eyes. 'I saw you watching us together. You looked—gutted.'

Gutted? 'No.' Cassie found a brief wry smile from somewhere. 'Come to my senses, more like.' She turned to face him fully, slender arms crossing her ribcage as she leant back against the unit behind her. 'What is your family going to say about you turning up in Florence, married to me and the father of five-year-old twins?'

'My family?' The hooded look altered into a frown.

'Gio mentioned at the restaurant the other night that you have a large family,' Cassie enlightened. 'He said you're good with families because you have a large one yourself.'

'I have a mother, two older sisters and my brother, Marco—I don't understand your drift.'

Cassie gave a shrug. 'Except for your brother you've never mentioned them to me, not once. Not in the past or in the present. I was wondering if there was a reason for that.'

'We have been dealing with us. I believed that was complicated enough.'

'Will they be at our wedding?'

Infinitesimally, he tensed. 'No. I felt it was best to keep the ceremony small and private in respect of the twins. I…could not be sure how they were going to feel about me.' He sketched out a brief smile. 'I did not know if I was going to have to drag you anchored to my wrist to marry me.'

Pressing her lips together, Cassie nodded, accepting that he had a point. The emotional ride they'd been travelling on for the last two weeks had not been conducive to social introductions;

even Angus would agree with that, since he'd been dragged onto the ride with them for a while.

'Your family knows about your blackouts?'

This time his tension was more obvious. 'Would you like to get where you're going with this, *cara*, because I am lost.'

Cassie wished she knew but she didn't. Something was nagging at her but she couldn't quite work out what that something was. 'I suppose it bothers me that we don't really know anything about each other,' she said as she tried to sort her own head out. 'Yet here we are, planning to get married like two reckless teenagers—'

'The evidence of our two five-year-old children hijacks the teenager part of that,' Sandro mocked.

'That's just arithmetic,' she dismissed. 'I still don't know you and you can't even remember me. The twins deserve a stable family environment. They don't deserve a set of parents who marry in haste for their so-called benefit, only to repent their decision later in front of them.'

'I will not regret marrying you,' Sandro stated firmly.

Cassie took in a breath. 'Well, I think we should wait.'

'No,' he refuted and now he was really uptight, hands out of his pockets and clenched.

'I think it would be kinder to the twins in the long run if we—'

'No!' he repeated with an angry rasp. 'I want marriage and I want it now. The twins expect it and I will not let you ruin what I am trying to build up with them! What the hell has got into you in the half an hour since we made love to each other?'

What had happened? Well, there was a clever question, Cassie thought unhappily. Then it hit, the nitty-gritty of what was bothering her.

'You made the assumption that I've had a string of lovers coming into this apartment,' she told him. 'If you knew me better you would know I would never do that in front of my children—'

'Our children—'

'And I don't like the way you voiced that assumption as if it didn't matter to you if I had introduced the twins to a long line of passing-through *uncles*. What do you think that tells me about your casual attitude to sex?'

'I don't do casual sex!' he denounced angrily,

then took in a deep breath. By the time he let the air back out of his lungs again he had shot down the short length of the kitchen so he was standing directly in front of her, his hand coming up to cup her cheek. 'Any woman with experience would know a man doesn't fall apart as I do with you if he was putting it out there like a damn stud,' he imparted huskily. 'You, *mi amore*, are not a woman of experience. Therefore my comment earlier was crude and unwarranted. I apologise for making it.'

Her intake of air ready to speak was stopped by the gentle pressure of his fingers against her lips. 'No,' he said. 'Just shut up and stop looking for excuses to get rid of me. We all belong together—remember that leap of faith.'

Was that what she was doing—looking for excuses to get rid of him? Searching his frowning dark eyes, Cassie decided that yes, she probably was. What kept on flaring up between them scared her. It seemed to happen with no reason or sense.

'You want me. I want you. We can work on the rest,' he said firmly. 'Trust me. Trust yourself. We both want this.'

This, she discovered, was the kind of slow, gentle kiss that muddied her brain up. This, was his hands gently stroking her face. It wasn't sexual, it wasn't even close to it. It was tender and reassuring and…oh, God, she just fell into it like a needy fool, pushing her niggles aside— once again.

CHAPTER TEN

SANDRO stayed with them at the flat until the twins were tucked up in bed and asleep. He'd raided the fridge and cooked them all pasta, turning the whole thing into a family event in which everyone was expected to participate.

And he did it with a smooth, flirtatious light-heartedness that papered over the cracks in his own splintered veneer. Cassie had shaken him when she'd gone back to questioning their marriage. He hadn't been expecting it; now his conscience was troubling him because he'd asked her to trust him when he knew her instincts were not playing her false.

'I will come back first thing in the morning,' he promised, drawing the words along her delicate jawline with the warmth of his breath.

'You could stay…'

He could stay. The soft invitation came with

the sinuous move of her body against his. For the first time she was coming on to him and he knew, with fierce regret, he had to push her away.

'No.' He softened the sting out of his refusal by claiming her ready mouth with his. 'We get married in less than thirty-six hours. No more sex before then. I've got standards,' he informed her loftily.

Cassie widened those velvet-green eyes, the tightly moulding front of her jeans pressing up against him. He wanted her and denying it was useless when the evidence was so on show.

'I will not confuse the twins by being the first man they find in your bed before we're married,' he determined, using the words to tell her that he still regretted making that earlier quip about her other lovers.

'Very honourable,' she praised him mock-solemnly, 'although you could creep out of here before sunrise…'

Using the spread of his hands to pull her even closer, 'Not so honourable,' he admitted, 'more a case of being aware that the walls in here are paper-thin and you can be—noisy.'

He grinned at the becoming blush that spread

into her cheeks. 'I won't have time to see you tomorrow,' she said. 'I have too many things I need to do.'

'I thought we were going shopping.' Sandro frowned down at her.

'For my wedding clothes? I think that's one small chore you can trust me to pull off without your input.'

'You mean you're shutting me out in punishment because I won't let you drag me back to bed.'

The spark that hit her eyes told him he was right. He released a sigh, then added a soft laugh. Beautiful, he thought as he looked down at her. Shy, feisty, stubborn, sexy. Intelligent, independent—and almost his.

And he had to get out of here before he burnt his boats, gave in and told her everything. Honourable? No. Ruthless and manipulative and calculating? Yes, he was all of those things. Plus a coward, for not daring to take a risk by trusting her with what he knew.

Combing his long fingers into her hair, he tilted her head back, the burning heat of his kiss telling her what he really wanted to do, before he was muttering a husky goodnight and getting out while he still could.

Cassie closed the door and leant into it with a silly, dreamy smile on her face. She took that smile into her bedroom and slept with it, woke up the next morning with it still in place. After delivering the twins to school she spent the rest of the day rushing around putting her affairs in order in readiness for her move to Florence.

By the time she arrived back at her flat, she was too tired to do much more than drop into the lumpy old armchair with her purchases piled around her aching feet. The telephone sitting on the bookcase by the chair started ringing. Smiling because she thought it must be Sandro calling her, she reached out to pick it up, but it wasn't Sandro.

'OK, let's have it,' Ella's voice came streaming down the line at her. 'Did you know our gorgeous boss was involved in a serious car accident around the time he got you pregnant with the twins?'

Sighing, Cassie sank more deeply into the chair. 'Yes.'

There was a short, sharp pause before Ella murmured, 'You're a dark horse, Cassie Janus.

I called him a rake on the take yesterday and you went out of your way to deny it, when all along you knew the guy's fiancée died in the same accident! He left you to go back to her, didn't he? You weren't just a babe in the arms of that handsome rat, you were the rejected third of a sleazy love triangle. No wonder he hit the floor when he saw you again—his damn guilty conscience sent him there!'

Cassie was floundering in a dizzy world of too much traumatic information. For several seconds she believed she was going to be the one to black out.

'Come on, Cassie—give!' Ella's voice spiked her eardrum.

'H-how did you get to hear about this?' she whispered.

'BarTec's buzzing with it,' Ella enlightened. 'It's even on Facebook! That vindictive bitch Pandora put it there!'

The phone rang again five minutes later. Cassie was still sitting in the chair. This time when she picked up the receiver it was Sandro.

'Cassie…' he said urgently.

He knew. He'd been warned.

'I hate you,' she whispered and put down the phone.

Sandro had been engaged to marry someone else when he'd pursued her in Devon. He'd used a different name so he couldn't be found out and all that rubbish about two names had been just a cover-up. He'd lied to her and he'd betrayed his fiancée.

Had she had an old Italian name like Sandro? Had she been beautiful? Had she been lovely and sweet and innocent and nice? Had she died, unaware that her fiancé had cheated on her? Was she allowed to cling to that small hope at least?

Like someone trapped in a daze, she got up from the chair and walked over to the cabinet where her laptop was housed when she wasn't using it. Five minutes later she was sitting at the dining table, staring at the most beautiful, dark-haired creature she had ever seen. Her eyes were blue, her smile was warm, and she was standing next to Sandro with his arm securing her to his side.

…Alessandro Marchese Rossi, the eldest son and heir to Italian industrialist Luciano Marchese, and Phebe Pyralis, the only daughter of the Greek industrialist Anton Pyralis, celebrating their engagement, which forges an alliance destined to set the industrial world on its ears…

She didn't want to read on but like a fool she just couldn't stop herself. There were photos and articles about the glittering couple, links to reports on the accident she couldn't bring herself to click on. Then her own face was suddenly looking back at her from a picture taken at the restaurant, followed by a damning exposure which placed Cassie as Sandro's secret lover at the time his fiancée had been killed. The existence of the twins was mentioned, followed by the assumption that their affair had taken place virtually beneath Angus's roof, though nothing could be further from the truth. If she'd met Sandro through Angus she would have known all about him and there would have been no affair— and ultimately no twins.

Nausea took a sudden hold of her, sending her lurching to her feet and rushing for the bathroom, but she didn't make it there because someone put their fingers on her doorbell, keeping it pealing like a Klaxon in her throbbing head and forcing her to go and answer it even though she didn't want to see or speak to anyone.

Sandro was standing there. He looked different—tough strains of tension locked onto the taut contours of his face.

'OK,' he spoke quickly. 'I should have told you.'

A strangled sob and Cassie tried to shut the door in his face. His hand snaking out to slam against the wood stopped her so she spun around and walked away. She heard the door click into its housing as she took up position in front of the casement window.

He followed her into the room, filling the doorway. She found her eyes grazing down his full length, dressed to its usual impeccable high standards in a steel-grey silk suit. He looked what he was, she thought bitterly, a lean, sleek sexual predator with a ruthless streak that cut right through to the core of him.

His angry eyes flicked around the room as if looking for something.

'They're not here,' Cassie told him. 'If they had been I would not have let you in.'

He shifted his tense, wide shoulders as if

shaking off her cold stricture, his gaze alighting on the laptop standing open on the table where she'd left it. Grim lips biting together, he strode over to it and with a touch from a long finger made the screen leap into life. His stillness clawed at her raw nerve-endings as she watched him watch his own history roll across the screen. The glittering betrothal, the tragic car accident, then the final exposure of her role in his life and the twins.

Wrapping her arms around her body, she tightened them until her ribs hurt. 'You turned me into the other woman and I didn't even know it,' she whispered.

'I'm sorry,' he murmured.

'I don't want to hear you tell me you're sorry!' Like a wounded animal she went on the attack. 'I just want you to tell me why you lied to me!'

'I did not lie.' Reaching out, he closed the laptop.

'Oh, I forgot, you don't remember me.' Her sarcasm hit a nerve because he turned on her then.

'All right!' he flung at her. 'So I've known since the first night we met again *why* I had forgotten you! Guilt is why I wiped you out of my head, Cassie! Sheer, gut-crucifying guilt!'

Hearing him actually voice the stark, crawling

truth of it drained the blood from her head. Sandro didn't look as if he was feeling any better. He was standing there rigid, looking as stunned as she was by his own confession.

His *guilty* confession! It was no wonder he kept on blacking out—he couldn't live with himself! This big, strong, dynamic male with the body of a warrior and the machinating mind of a general had learnt the hardest way possible that he actually possessed a conscience!

'You bastard,' she breathed with the frailest flimsiness because she didn't dare test the strength of her voice against what was backing up behind it.

'*Sí*,' he agreed.

'The way you treat w-women, I can actually understand why Pandora did what she did!'

He stiffened his backbone. 'What is that supposed to imply?'

'Hell has no fury,' Cassie supplied with thick, tremulous mockery. 'She was your lover before I came along. You must have—'

'She was not my lover.'

'What was she, then?'

'My assistant,' he said. 'My—'

'*Personal* assistant?'

'No!' he raked out. 'And quit with the sarcasm,' he growled impatiently. 'My relationship with Pandora is purely professional! *OK*...' He sighed out harshly when he read her expression. 'So I knew she had...feelings for me. I decided to do something about it to help her get over her...infatuation, by removing her out of my sphere and putting her in charge of BarTec while I turned my attention to other things! She did not like it but she did look forward to the challenge so accepted the opportunity! Then you came crashing back into my life, and it's clear now that she allowed her feelings for me to override her professional common sense!'

'Did you ever sleep with her?'

'No.'

'Did you ever *want* to sleep with her?'

'No!' he bit out. 'If you want the truth, she had become a pain in the damn neck! When Gio told me she was giving you a hard time at BarTec, I decided it was time I did something more permanent about her...emotional attachment, so I sent her back to Florence with notice to find herself another job. This…' the laptop was waved at '…was her vindictive response!'

'OK,' Cassie whispered. 'I believe you.'

'*Grazie,*' he responded with stiff-necked thinness, not in the least bit happy about being put on the rack about Pandora in the first place.

'Don't think for one second that I forgive you for any of it!' She instantly fired up. '*You* should have told me about your f-fiancée, Sandro!'

'I tried to several times but…' he stopped to sigh then pushed his fingers through his hair '…I knew it was going to hurt you. And I could not predict how you were going to react. So I decided to wait until we were safely married before I explained about—about Phebe.' He couldn't even say her name without swallowing first! 'And I also had to think about what was best for the twins.'

'Don't you *dare* bring them into this!' Cassie choked out. 'And I am not in the least bit impressed by your excuses! Right from the start it's always been what you decided. What you wanted to do! Well, what about me and what I might have wanted?'

'You wanted me,' he declared harshly. 'From

the moment you looked at me in that damn res-taurant, Cassie, you—wanted—me! Well, now you have me, tied, trussed and bloody gift-wrapped! I'm *giving* you what you wanted!'

'Y-you conceited devil!' she gasped.

'I wanted you the same way. Why deny it that we *both* want the same thing?'

'I did not want to be the cross you've decided to bear to salve your lousy guilty conscience!'

She hated him for turning her into that—she would hate him forever for it!

'Did she—your fiancée know about me?' she spun at him chokily.

'No,' he roughed out.

One tiny chink of relief in a black storm of shame and misery, Cassie thought painfully.

'She came to meet me at the airport the day I left here,' he continued heavily. 'We hit an oil spill on the way into Florence. She—died later…' He took another thick pause for several long seconds before he added, 'I think that's all you need to know.'

Cassie nodded as a sickly quiver of muddled emotions riddled her insides. She felt sorry for poor, tragic, beautiful Phebe Pyralis. She even felt a pang of sorrow for Sandro and what he had lost that night. A six-week black hole in his memory seemed like nothing now when held up against the vivid images he had just sketched out.

Two people, a car, an oil slick, two broken bodies... Her hand went up to cover her mouth. Two lives shattered in the skidding grind of twisting metal. Three more lives—her own and the twins'—spinning off into the black hole Sandro's mind had become.

'"*I don't know you. I don't want to know you,*"' she whispered. 'No wonder you said those words to me.' His brain had refused to let him remember her on any level, even her cry for help.

He threw back his shoulders, his fabulous bone structure fiercely pronounced. 'What I said to you that day was—*is*—unforgivable,' he accepted tautly. 'All I can say in my defence is that I did not remember you. And Phebe...' he stopped to swallow, his expression raw and ravaged '...Phebe and I were both left in deep comas after the accident. She—she did not come through it... I did...'

Raw agony scored his elegant cheekbones—

survivor guilt, Cassie recognised, feeling the pain with him, though she wished that she didn't.

'The day you made that call to me was the same day we buried her…' he went on once he found the control to do so. 'It was, *cara*, the worst day of my life.'

Oh, dear God… Cassie spun away again, her hand jerking back up to cover her mouth. Nothing—nothing she had been feeling back then had felt as bad as this did right now.

'I was in a mess,' Sandro continued starkly. 'I was barely functioning as a human being. I don't remember deleting your calls from my mobile's memory, and know now that I blocked them out afterwards as I had blocked out everything else about you…'

Cassie closed her eyes, trying to think past the strangle of emotions twisting around inside her and couldn't. She hurt for poor Phebe. She hurt for Sandro, for herself and the twins.

'When we met again—'

'Please,' Cassie whispered. 'Don't say anything else.'

She'd heard enough—*understood* enough. Phebe, poor, beautiful Phebe, had been Sandro's real love and he'd cheated on her. Blocking out everything about her had been the only way he could live with his guilt. That did not make him a bad man, just a—a flawed one.

For six long years she had seen herself as Sandro's sleazy one-night stand. Learning about his accident and his lost memory had given her back her dignity, the right to lift herself up from that lowly place. Now here she was, sunk right back down in the sleaze by the introduction of the beautiful Phebe Pyralis, who, if she had not died in that wretched car accident, would be blissfully married to Sandro by now, probably surrounded by the gift of their own children, and she and the twins would still be cast out of his life like unwanted garbage.

Instead, and because of a trick of fate, she had been offered the star prize in Phebe Pyralis's stead: marriage to Sandro. A father for her children. *Great*, she thought emptily. *Aren't I the lucky one*?

Compared to Phebe Pyralis—yes, a cold little voice inside her said.

Her tormented dark eyes fixed on the array of bags and boxes still lying where she'd dropped them by the chair. Her stomach began cramping again when she caught herself listing what was inside them—her carefully chosen bridal outfit aimed at romance because that reflected exactly how she had felt. A pretty dress for Bella aimed to fulfil her daughter's fairy-tale expectations. An outfit she'd hoped was going to pass Anthony's critical ideas about what a five-year-old boy would wear to a wedding.

A wedding.

On a clutch of raw hurt she swung her back to Sandro and closed her eyes as they began to sting.

'Cassie…'

She shook her head to silence him. 'I want you to leave now,' she whispered. 'The twins will be home soon. I would prefer it if you weren't here when they arrive.'

Silence met that, a long, taut, pulsating silence that forced her eyes open and made her turn to look at him. His dark head was back, his squared chin jutted, the whole repertoire of his handsome arrogance etched in gold marble on his face. His eyes were burning. His mouth drawn flat. There wasn't a bone in his magnificent body that wasn't stretched and locked. The sheer physical power in his pulsing tension made the room seem to darken and shrink.

'You're chucking me out,' he breathed through his tightly clenched teeth.

'Wh-what did you expect me to do,' Cassie countered, 'just shrug it all off and carry on as we were?'

The way he seemed to vibrate where he stood made her wonder if that was exactly what he expected of her. 'You believe you can wrench my children from my arms and walk away with them!'

'M-my children too.' *Wrench* from his arms…? 'And I don't recall saying I would do that!'

'It's what you're thinking!' he charged angrily. 'You want to punish me! You want to dismiss me from your life!'

'Isn't that what you did to me six years ago?'

As if she'd struck him right below the belt, Sandro reeled on his heels and swung away from her. As she stood there, watching him bunch and flex his impressive shoulder muscles, Cassie wished that she had! She wished he would drop into one of his blackouts so she could just…step over him and walk out!

'Just go, Sandro.' She spun away again. 'I can't *cope* with any more from you right now.'

Her hand jerked up to cover her mouth again. She was a mess. Her insides were a mess, trembling and fluttering, her limbs were shaking, her heart grabbing only the occasional thick beat.

Behind her another thick, brooding silence began to suck the oxygen out of the atmosphere. In front of her she watched as the first spots of rain hit the window. The skies had darkened while they'd been fighting, bringing a two-week Indian summer to an abrupt ending. Now the twins will get wet, was the one hazy thought to enter her head.

A sound of sudden movement behind her made her tense sharply and turn. Sandro was closing the gap between them, and she did not like the look on his face as he did. Acting on pure impulse, Cassie made a dive for cover behind the sofa because something in him had changed—his *mood* had changed.

Electric sensation fizzed up through her blood. 'Don't you dare come near me!' she choked out.

As if the sofa was going to stop him, she mocked her mode of defence when all he did was grab hold of it and shift it out of his path, forcing her backwards until her shoulders hit the wall behind.

'Wh-wh-what do you think you're doing?' Her clenched hands jerked up to push at his chest when he just kept on coming, making her slender arms bend until her fists were crushed between her breasts and his rock-solid chest. She'd never known him behave so physically threateningly, never seen that strange, burning look in his eyes. She wondered if she should be scared, but she wasn't scared, she was—

'I am about to check if you can cope with any more from me,' he teethed out, then speared his long fingers into her hair and used them to tilt back her head.

Her tear-spiked eyelashes trembled and her breathing feathered as the full, unfair, determined beauty of him swam close. 'I don't want—'

The rest was lost—stolen from her by the marauding pressure of his mouth and the pillaging invasion of his tongue. Her defences tumbled like poorly constructed blocks. Her clenched fingers straightened out then clutched at his shirt.

Her limbs turned to liquid. Her wretched, traitorous body filled with desire. He explored her mouth with a sensual expertise that won her hungry response. It just wasn't fair, she thought helplessly as his grimly determined seduction spilled over into mindless passion and she gave herself up to it.

When he finally eased the agony of it and lifted his head to look into her dazed, glazed eyes, his soft and taunting, 'You can cope, *cara*. You can cope with a hell of a lot more from me,' made her cringe in shame.

Releasing his grip on her, he turned away and strode back across the room. 'I will see you at our wedding venue tomorrow at eleven-thirty.' He even calmly straightened the sofa as he went. 'Don't be late.'

'I won't be there.' Cassie's arms were back like bands around her shaking body.

'You will be there,' he countered. 'You cannot afford not to turn up.'

Catching her breath, she stared at him. 'What's that supposed to mean?'

He'd reached the door by now. A tall, dark, lethal example of male arrogance steeped in unshakable self-confidence. Making the half-turn he required to look at her, ice-shot, ink-black eyes fixed on her pale face, his whole cool attitude and taut, elegant stature declaring that he was firmly back in control here, armed and ready to take on the fight.

'I own right of say over your monthly salary,' he reminded her with the smooth, calm thrust of a steely knife. 'Perhaps what you don't know is that I also own right of say over your reduced rent for this place. If you need confirmation of that, call Angus,' he suggested. 'He will tell you I bought his property portfolio at the same time I bought BarTec.'

Cassie's strangled gasp hurt her throat. She needed to stay leaning against the wall because her legs had gone hollow with shock. 'I suppose you've been dying to tell me that from the beginning,' she breathed hoarsely.

'On the contrary, I would have preferred not to play these cards with you.' The hard cast of his face took on a bleak, sardonic smile. 'However, we don't have enough time left to allow you to prevaricate while you…salve your wounded pride over something neither of us can do anything about.'

'What pride?' Cassie choked out. 'I don't have any. You've stripped me of it!'

Even the wall wasn't going to hold her up now, she realised as her hollow legs turned to jelly along with her queasy stomach, and her quivering heart. Almost stumbling like a blind woman she groped her way around the sofa and sat down on it, curling into the corner of it like a cowering whipped dog.

'Look…' he sighed, clearly not liking the whipped-dog look '…we have to—'

'Shut up. I hate you. Get out,' she whispered in fierce loathing.

'When someone breaks the rules they must expect to pay for it!' Sandro suddenly rasped out. 'Six years ago I broke the rules, but you have been the one paying for it. Now I must and I *will* repay that debt to you!'

He was talking about marriage again. But did he really believe that marrying her was *repaying* her for what he'd done? 'I will not be the cross for you to bear on your rotten guilt crusade!'

'That wasn't what I meant.'

'It's how it sounds!'

'All right, I will rephrase it.' He took in a deep breath. 'I broke the rules. The *twins* have been paying for it. Now it is time for me to repay my debt to *them*.'

'Well, that just about crowns the insults you've been piling on me, doesn't it?'

His answering sigh came with a frown that sent his fingers shooting up to his brow. Like someone riding on a see-saw of violently swaying emotions, Cassie felt the stomach-riddling clutch of her hatred switch to a heart-squeezing wrench of concern.

'Don't you dare black out on me, Sandro!' she launched at him furiously.

'I'm not—'

'Yes, you are!' On a groan of sizzling frustration Cassie unfolded her curled figure and rose to her feet.

She saw him tense as she approached him, then still when her fingers gripped his arm. Another second later and he was dropping his shoulders and swaying sideways to prop himself against the frame of the door.

'What caused it this time?' she questioned reluctantly.

He sketched out a half-smile. 'The sweet, loving tone of your voice?'

'Don't joke,' Cassie husked, her other hand already covering the thankfully steady beat of his heart. 'You need to sit down—'

'What I need is for you to stop fighting me.'

'And do what instead—forgive you for your sins?'

'*Sí.*' He dropped the hand from his face and looked at her, those deep-set dark eyes framed by unfairly long eyelashes reflecting a sombre beauty that clutched like a vice at her heart. 'You have bought the dress, *cara*—I saw the shopping. You know deep down you care about me.' Reaching up, he scored a thumb across her kiss-warmed, trembling mouth. 'Hate me later, after we marry. I will be able to deal with it better then.'

Cassie drew her head back, away from his caressing finger. 'And how can you be sure of that?'

He offered a tense smile. 'Call it instinct.'

Instinct, she mocked. What he was doing was playing tunes on her sympathy. He was ruthlessly jumping on her moment of weakness that had brought her over here to him! His brow still wore the ghost of a pained frown, his stance still relied heavily on the door frame. And his hand was covering her hand now, pressing it into the heated shirt stretched over his beating heart.

'I vow to you, on my own life, you will not regret it.'

Pressed, pushed, feeling the hurt again and aching with it, she snatched her hand away and walked back to the sofa to curl down into it, waging angry battles with herself now, as well as with him.

'Think what it will do to the twins if you pull back from me now.'

Her eyes slid to her pile of shopping. She did as he said and thought about the twins. They needed him now—*wanted* what he was offering them. She could not take their happiness away from them because she had deep problems with what Sandro was.

'I won't sleep in your bed.' The condition leapt from her lips without her knowing she was going to say it.

She didn't look up when, after a few seconds, Sandro said quietly, 'Fair enough,' and left the apartment without saying another word.

A tactical retreat from the conniving, lying, manipulating general, she recognised, not liking herself one little bit for weakening her stance against him.

CHAPTER ELEVEN

SANDRO glanced at his watch, his tension tangible as he paced the town-hall foyer like a jungle cat constrained in a cage. Happening to glance up, he glared at the two men who were standing watching him.

'Say a single word and I will hit the pair of you,' he growled as he put in a couple more restless strides.

'They are on their way,' Gio Rozario dared. 'The traffic is bad.'

'If you're this uncertain about her, Alessandro, then maybe you should think twice about—'

'You might be my brother and a damn good doctor, Marco, but you have no clue what it is you are talking about!' He swung around forcefully on his brother. 'So keep your damned opinion to yourself.'

The way Marco held his hands up in a gesture

of surrender and backed right off only made Sandro feel as if there was still a chance that he was going to lash out anyway.

He turned on his heel and strode back the way he had come. His brother had issues about what he was doing. But then, despite his medical training, Marco could not see what was going on inside his head. Marco could scan it, give an expert diagnosis on it, declare it perfectly healthy other than for a six-year-old scarring that would never go away. But he could not read its thoughts or the emotions that ranted through it—or the urgency that was driving him and, through him, Cassie into this marriage.

He'd waited six long, blacked-out years for this moment—for this woman to become his wife.

'The car has arrived,' Gio said quietly.

Swinging round to stride back to the doorway, Sandro was in time to watch his driver lift Bella out of the car and set her down on the pavement at the bottom of the town-hall steps and felt a hand grab hold of his heart then close into a fist. His beautiful, golden-haired daughter looked the perfect image of her own idea of how a princess should look in a frivolously pretty pink dress.

Cassie had done that—fulfilled Bella's dream for her, though she did not want the dream for herself.

His son arrived next, scrambling out of the car under his own steam to immediately start jumping on the bottom stone step. He was wearing jeans and trainers and a blue and red checked shirt. His son's mother had not made the mistake of offending the small boy's dignity by dressing him in fancy wedding clothes.

That fist around his heart tightened its grip.

Then tightened some more as he watched a pair of slender, very female legs slide out of the car, followed by the rest of this beautiful creature who was his reluctant bride. She was wearing white, a silky white skirt that floated around her slender knees and a lacy jacket that nipped her tiny waist. Strappy white high-heeled shoes elevated her delicate ankles, and she'd dressed her hair up with a single pink-petalled rose.

He watched her look up, watched her go still, watched her dense, dark, fabulous green eyes flutter a glance down his full length. His body fired up, his tension levels along with it.

Cassie found herself pinned to the pavement by

an all-over sensation of prickly heat. From down here at the bottom of the steps Sandro looked taller than he really was, and darker than he really was, and ten times more stunningly attractive than she wanted to believe that he was. His suit was black, beautiful, devastatingly elegant, his shirt so white it blinded her in the sun. Skin like warm olives, eyes as dark as pits and powerfully intense, his mouth so arrogantly firm yet so inherently sensual her lips gave a sting in recognition of what his could do to them.

She had to lower her eyes before she could make herself move again, her slender-heeled shoes suddenly feeling too fragile to support the odd new whirlpool heaviness that had taken over her legs. The twins were already running up the steps towards him, shouting out to him, expecting and receiving the kind of warm, smiling welcome they'd already become used to receiving from him.

Cassie followed at a slower pace, aware that she should not be doing this—did not *want* to be doing this, yet every nerve-ending she had was urging her onward as if Sandro was drawing her there with his indomitable will.

Bella was doing twirls for him, Anthony tugging on one of his hands while telling him something she didn't think Sandro heard because his attention was still fixed on her. And her heart was pounding, the knowledge that she should not be feeling anything for him acting like a tormenting sting in her throat. When she reached the top of the step and was finally forced to lift her chin and look up at him, that all-over feeling of prickly heat changed to a quivering wash of helpless female awareness she wished so badly she didn't feel.

Dense, dark brown eyes grabbed hold of her eyes. He reached for her hands and lifted them to his lips. 'You look sensational,' he told her.

Then Ella came running up the steps, looking harassed and breathless. 'Sorry I'm late. The traffic is crazy…'

And her friend's arrival saved Cassie from saying something stupid back to Sandro like—so do you.

Sandro picked up the polite duties of host, introducing everyone to each other—one of her hands held firmly trapped in his.

Marco sent her a brief wry smile. 'It is a pleasure to meet you properly at last.'

But was it? Cassie found herself questioning as she laid her free hand in his. There was something restrained about his smile and his manner and even his tone of voice. Did he disapprove of her? Was he comparing her with the beautiful Phebe Pyralis and finding her lacking? Was he thinking about her and Sandro's past association as he drew his hand from hers and turned away to greet her friend?

Her throat went so dry she couldn't even swallow. Finding a smile for Gio Rosario actually hurt her tense mouth. When the registrar appeared to invite them to follow her, Cassie froze so totally she had a horrible feeling she might just be going to faint.

Great cop-out but—yes, please, she begged silently.

Then Sandro was feeding his hand across her tense back, his long fingers curving into her waist. He urged her forward, his own grim, silent tension telling her that he was aware she was still fighting with herself about going through with this.

'My reluctant bride,' he drawled sardonically as his car sped them away towards the airport, leaving Gio and Ella standing on the town-hall steps, planning where to have lunch. Sandro's brother had excused himself and rushed off directly after the ceremony was over, claiming a heavy work schedule.

Cassie wondered if the word *'ceremony'* covered what had been just thirty short minutes of soulless promises before she was elevated from plain Cassie Janus to the super-elegant Mrs Alessandro Marchese.

'When you lost your voice halfway through your declaration, I half expected someone to stride through the doors and announce you were not lawfully free to marry me,' Sandro mocked.

Her quick-witted daughter had come to her rescue. Bella had tugged on her skirt and whispered, 'You haven't finished yet, Mummy,' while everyone else had begun shifting their stance.

I, Cassie Janus, take Alessandro Marchese...

No wonder she'd frozen up. She'd finally been forced to refer to him by that name.

'Look at the way your ring is sparkling, Mummy,' Bella piped up, reminding them both that the twins were travelling with them.

The perfect killers of adult conversation, Cassie mused with a smile at the twins. She glanced down at the sparkling diamond ring slotted on her finger next to the wedding ring which matched the one she'd almost dropped to the floor, she'd been trembling so badly as she'd tried to slot it on Sandro's long, brown, rock-steady finger.

Sandro reached across the twins' heads and stroked one of those long fingers down her pale cheek. He didn't speak. When she glanced up at his face he still said nothing, but there was a possessive glow burning in his dark eyes that spread a warm flush right through her tense body.

His wife, her husband—for better and for worse now that the deed had been done. And the reason for that sat here between them, a small boy and girl wearing happy, contented faces.

Oh, come off it, Cassie, she then told herself impatiently. In the end and no matter what you've been fighting or thinking or saying— you're exactly where you want to be right now!

The sun was beginning to set by the time they sank through the air in a sweeping circle around the kind of house and gardens that took Cassie's breath away.

To reach this far they'd travelled by private jet to Vespucci Airport in Florence, then transferred to one of Sandro's private helicopters to make the sixty-kilometre trip south to arrive here, at the Marchese private country estate.

The twins were tired, the bubble of overexcitement which had carried them through the start of their long journey chiselled away by too many hours of confinement, and they were unimpressed by this first view of their new home.

On the other hand Cassie was beginning to truly realise just what kind of man it was she had married. She had known the Sandro of six years ago had come from money by his air of self-assurance, the quality of his clothes and the kind of flashy red sports car he had driven her around in then. When she'd met him again two weeks ago, she'd had to push him further up the moneyed ranking because of the sheer nature of who he had become as the controlling head of Marchese Industries.

However, this huge square stone villa with its apricot stuccoed walls blushing warmly in the dying sunlight, surrounded by the kind of gardens you usually only saw in travel magazines, pushed him even further up the rankings to a place beyond her present ability to comprehend.

'Welcome to the Villa Marchese,' he murmured as they settled down on the ground. 'What do you think?' he asked Cassie curiously.

'It's—big,' was all she could find to say.

'It's not a castle,' their daughter said in disappointment.

'So I can't please anyone today.' Sandro sighed out whimsically.

'I saw a huge swimming pool,' Anthony chipped in. 'Can we swim in it now?'

'Except for my son—a little,' Sandro added ruefully.

Opening the door, he climbed down then turned to lift the twins out. As though they'd been set free from a cage, they ran off towards the villa, putting Cassie's heart into a fluttering panic because she had never let them move so far away from her before.

'Sandro, catch them!' she cried in alarm, moving without thinking what she was doing, so when she swung her legs out of the helicopter and went to lower herself to the ground she discovered the scary way that she was much higher up than she'd realised.

By then it was already too late, and that first impulsive move continued to carry her forward. Her heart gave a thump, that fizzing feeling you got when you knew you were going to fall washing agitated tingles down her legs, and she let out a frightened yelp.

Spinning around, Sandro ripped out a soft curse then came to her rescue, his strong arms banding around her body and gathering her up to hold her securely flattened to his long, hard length. Without even thinking about it, Cassie flung her arms around his neck and clung on for dear life.

'I knew you would fall for me all over again once you'd seen my house,' he said lazily.

'It isn't a joke!' Firing a shaken look up at him, Cassie caught the smiling glint of his white teeth—the genuine laughter that reflected in his eyes. The dying sunlight was bronzing his fabulous features, his smooth forehead, his vibrant cheekbones, his jawline, the glowing patina of health that glossed his fleshless cheeks. Finally she collided with those sizzling gold flecks sparkling in his eyes, and that sinking feeling shot through her for a second time, only this one was down to the dizzying swoop of her own aching emotions, fighting against the hard, cold clutch of reality that he'd used her terribly six years ago for a one-night stand.

'Put me down,' she instructed.

And watched the laughter die. Instead of setting her feet to the ground he strengthened the muscles in his arms. She saw what was coming, and her fingertips curled tensely into his shirt collar.

'Sandro, no,' she jerked out.

'*Dio*, Sandro, yes,' he delivered in a deep voice roughened by his intentions, and lifted her higher at the same time as he lowered his dark head to capture her mouth.

And he took it with a fire-hot hunger. The old electric excitement dragging a helpless whimper from her in response. With a muffled groan of raw desire he drove his tongue deep into her mouth on a passionately sensual exploration that blew her defences wide apart. Her head fell back against his shoulder; her heart began to pound. It was dreadful and wonderful at the same time, because she needed this kiss so badly it was no use trying to kid herself any more.

She wanted him. She was hungry for him, confused and mad and wild—and she kissed him back with every bit of singing, pulsing, throbbing passion that she had in her, yet aching tears filled her eyes when he finally allowed their mouths to part so they could draw breath.

'You should have told me about her,' she sobbed out painfully.

'I couldn't.' His voice sounded harsh, thick, unsteady. 'I'd hurt you too much already by abandoning you. I could not hurt you again by telling you about her.'

'You loved her—'

'No,' he denied fiercely, banding her more tightly to him. 'We did not have that kind of relationship. She was my friend before she became my betrothed. We kind of drifted into the idea of marriage because it suited our two families but—*damn*,' he husked, 'she was *nice*!'

Cassie shivered, wondering how he would have felt if poor Phebe had described him as just *nice*.

'I loved her, but not in the way I should have done. I know that now but I did not understand then,' he breathed raggedly. 'She did not need my money because she had her own money. She did not need me to elevate her place in society because she already had that too. She did not expect great passion from me and she did not mind that I was more into work than being romantic.'

'If you're about to confess that the two of you made love by appointment then I don't want to hear about it,' Cassie sparked up brokenly.

'We never made love! *Hell—damn...!*' Setting her down on her feet, he fell into a rage of Italian curses while Cassie stood trembling and stared at him in stinging disbelief.

There was just no way she was going to believe that one, knowing the depth and strength of his passions the way she did!

'Before I left to come to England, we had even talked about calling our engagement off!' he delivered harshly. 'Because our betrothal was so high-profile we decided we should use the time I was away to think about it before we decided to cause some pretty heavy family waves.'

'That's a lousy let-out—'

'You bet it's a lousy let-out!' Sandro agreed forcefully. 'Do you think I'm not aware of that?' he demanded. 'Do you think I am not aware that the moment I set foot on British soil and saw you, I was using that damned excuse like some kind of mantra that absolved me of sin? Do you think I am not also aware that I shut all memory of you out because that had to be my punishment for wanting you more than I wanted her?'

'Y-you think you killed her, I can understand that, but—'

'What are you talking about?' His head shot back, gold-flecked dark eyes pinning her with a stunned stare. 'I didn't kill Phebe—she almost killed me! *She* was driving the car! Didn't you read the stuff about the accident Pandora put on Facebook?'

Eyelashes trembling, Cassie shook her head. 'I w-was scared there would be photographs of your injuries.'

'There were.' Sandro swallowed tensely. 'It took them hours to cut us out of the car. For myself I don't remember anything about it and I have only thin sketches of what came before. But I remember that Phebe was tense, distracted, telling me something—' he lifted his fingers to his brow '—I can't remember what, but I can see her tension—feel it. But I blamed it on my own tension because I knew I had to tell her about you, then—*Dio*,' he swore when he saw the tears running down Cassie's cheeks. 'Don't you dare weep on me, *cara*,' he warned, 'or I will not be responsible for what happens next, or *where* it happens!'

Cassie controlled the tears with an inelegant sniff. Sandro muttered something else in Italian then stepped in close to ravage her soft, quivering mouth.

'You—'

'Just shut up,' he groaned when she tried to speak again, his next kiss bruising her mouth as if he wanted to punish her for thinking at all. 'Can't you tell when a man is crazy about you?' he demanded roughly. 'Is it not enough that you embarrassed me when you made me drop like a stone at your feet?'

'Your guilty conscience did that—'

'*You* did that!' he countered fiercely. His eyes were fierce, the way he was crushing her to him again was fierce. 'You, with your beautiful green eyes spitting hell at me—*you*!'

They were still standing on the gravel platform built to take the helicopter. Neither had noticed that the pilot had quietly slipped away or that their children's voices had faded, or that the grey-framed windows in the apricot-stuccoed villa were lined with interested faces.

But Cassie remembered the children now. 'Sandro, the twins have disappeared!' A flare of alarm set her wriggling in his arms.

He pulled her back again. 'There is an army of staff employed here, every one of them capable of watching over two children without my having to relinquish what I have here.'

'And what do you have?' Cassie looked at him.

'A wife,' he said. 'My woman, shackled to me in more ways than one.' The tension in his arms made sure she was aware of at least one other way she was shackled to him. 'You love me. You're as crazy about me as I am about you. Why don't you give in and just tell me so I can relax my guard and move this on?'

A small frown puckered the top of Cassie's nose as she continued to look at him. Her teeth fastened into her kiss-swollen bottom lip. He was shamelessly arrogant, and shamelessly sure of himself. But…there was something else about him that was niggling at her right now.

'Move this on where?' she asked cautiously.

His tense mouth broke into a wry kind of smile. 'Well, not to a girly pink bed, that's for sure,' he drawled.

And that was it—the thing that had been nagging at the back of her mind right through this whole heated conversation. 'You've remembered everything!' she choked out.

'Mmm,' he smiled.

'Why didn't you tell me?'

'Because I needed to hang on to your sympathetic side until I had you caught, tethered and incarcerated here,' he explained. 'Allowing you to believe I was going to drop to the ground whenever we had a fight made your defences crumble.'

'But that's—'

'Sneaky, devious, underhand?' Sandro suggested.

'When?' she demanded. 'When did you remember?'

'At Angus's house….' he said without a single hint of remorse. 'I spent the next three days in my brother's care while my head bombarded me with six forgotten weeks of pure hell and misery. Letting you continue to believe I was still struggling with flashbacks was the perfect diversion tactic to keep you focused on what really mattered.'

'Which was you, of course,' Cassie sighed out.

'And what you really felt about me,' Sandro extended.

The children came tearing around a corner of the house then, with several members of his staff in hot pursuit. From being travel-tired they'd suddenly found a new lease of energy that made Sandro sigh.

'I don't suppose you would like to tell me you love me before we have to break this off for a while…?' he murmured hopefully.

Not before you say it first, she thought.

'Mummy, you've just got to come and see how big this house is!' Anthony called out excitedly.

'It almost as big as a castle!' his twin enthused. 'And they—' Bella pointed towards the cluster of people standing back now that the twins had reached their parents '—won't let us jump in the swimming pool.'

'I don't think they understood us when we said we can swim,' Anthony explained.

'I think they did,' their father murmured indistinctly, then very casually to Cassie, 'I will punish you later for holding out on me,' he warned.

'Well, that sounds—interesting,' she responded primly.

And found herself scooped unceremoniously off the ground. 'Excuse us,' he said to their surprised assembly. 'We have a…tradition to get out of the way.'

Then while Cassie clung to him, red-faced, he sent the twins a reassuring smile. 'Your mother is…tired. I'm going to put her to bed. If you really want to swim, use the heated indoor pool—but not without at least two grown-ups to accompany you, got that?'

The twins nodded. So did Sandro, then he dealt out a smooth set of instructions to his hovering staff, which boiled down to them keeping the twins entertained and out of their way for an hour or two—or three—then he strode off towards the house with the sound of their children whooping as they turned their excited attention on the waiting staff.

'An outdoor *and* an indoor pool?' Cassie murmured in wonder.

'Impressed?' He glanced down at her.

She nodded. 'And these…traditions you mentioned?' she prompted.

'A threshold to negotiate,' he answered. 'A marriage bed to find. And a very large, disgustingly ostentatious, very, very sexy diamond necklace to unearth from my pocket. I have other traditions to attend to,' he added loftily, 'but they require a few special magic words to…set them in play.'

Staring up at his cool, dark features, Cassie slid her arms a little further around his wide shoulders. The tip of her tongue appeared to run a delicate line across her upper lip. The glossy thickness of his eyelashes folded downwards to watch the telling little action, then lift upwards again to pin her with a deadly look.

Sexy, unbearably sexy, Cassie thought as her pulse began to drum to a heavier beat. Sandro stopped walking. The tension heightened, simmering like electricity between them both.

'Well?' he prompted.

They were still standing out in the dying sunshine, the solid shape of the villa still several long strides away. Cassie moved in his arms, snaking that bit closer to the intimate lure of his stubborn mouth. 'You say it first.'

'What you really want is my beating heart laid out on a platter, don't you?' he murmured narrowly.

'Mmm,' Cassie confirmed. 'You see, I have these terrible words still rolling round my head I have not forgiven you for…'

She was referring to the telephone call. Sandro knew that, just as he knew what she was not saying here. He was going to have to work very hard to overwrite that piece of brutality.

'You have to know, *bella mia*, that those words were not spoken by the man you see standing here,' he imparted soberly. 'That guy lost himself six long, miserable years ago and only found himself when he set eyes on you again. If you think about it, that's a hell of a statement to make about loving you.'

Put like that, he was right, and it was one hell of a statement, Cassie acknowledged, vulnerable, river-green eyes floating over the solemn beauty of his face. Six years ago she'd fallen in love with Sandro Rossi. When she made that fatal phone call to him, a different, broken version of him had taken his place. Even when they met up again it was not that Sandro she'd fallen in love with but a guy called Alessandro Marchese—for once the different name started to make a mad kind of sense.

'OK,' she said softly, 'that's fair enough. So I love you too,' she returned unsteadily. 'I never stopped loving you throughout your six miserable lost years. I'm glad you found yourself again, Alessandro Marchese, and even more glad that you found me.'

The sober expression eased out of his features; a smile took its place. 'Now, that,' he said as he started walking again, 'deserves a reward.'

'Mmm,' Cassie said, making herself more comfortable in his arms, 'this sounds…interesting.'

The villa waited. Cassie didn't see any of its breathtaking beauty as Sandro carried her up the wide, curving staircase. She didn't even see the unapologetic baroque splendour of the bedroom he carried her into with its rich red velvet drapes and pale damask walls, and gilt-wood furniture set on a vast and glossy parquetry floor, or the huge bed he laid her on that was an extravagant vision hung on four corners with burnished gold silk.

She only saw the man as he came to stretch out beside her, dangling a gold chain from his long fingers with its totally ostentatious diamond droplet trailing across her mouth.

'I'm going to make love to you until you think you're dying,' Sandro murmured as if it was a soft, deep, sensual threat.

Parting her lips, Cassie licked the diamond. 'Oh, yes, please,' Cassie said.

MILLS & BOON PUBLISH EIGHT LARGE PRINT TITLES A MONTH. THESE ARE THE EIGHT TITLES FOR JANUARY 2010.

0110 Rom LP

MILLS & BOON PUBLISH EIGHT LARGE PRINT TITLES A MONTH. THESE ARE THE EIGHT TITLES FOR FEBRUARY 2010.

———————— ❧ ————————

DESERT PRINCE, BRIDE OF INNOCENCE
Lynne Graham

RAFFAELE: TAMING HIS TEMPESTUOUS VIRGIN
Sandra Marton

THE ITALIAN BILLIONAIRE'S SECRETARY MISTRESS
Sharon Kendrick

BRIDE, BOUGHT AND PAID FOR
Helen Bianchin

BETROTHED: TO THE PEOPLE'S PRINCE
Marion Lennox

THE BRIDESMAID'S BABY
Barbara Hannay

THE GREEK'S LONG-LOST SON
Rebecca Winters

HIS HOUSEKEEPER BRIDE
Melissa James

millsandboon.co.uk Community

Join Us!

The Community is the perfect place to meet and chat to kindred spirits who love books and reading as much as you do, but it's also the place to:

- **Get the inside scoop from authors about their latest books**
- **Learn how to write a romance book with advice from our editors**
- **Help us to continue publishing the best in women's fiction**
- **Share your thoughts on the books we publish**
- **Befriend other users**

Forums: Interact with each other as well as authors, editors and a whole host of other users worldwide.

Blogs: Every registered community member has their own blog to tell the world what they're up to and what's on their mind.

Book Challenge: We're aiming to read 5,000 books and have joined forces with The Reading Agency in our inaugural Book Challenge.

Profile Page: Showcase yourself and keep a record of your recent community activity.

Social Networking: We've added buttons at the end of every post to share via digg, Facebook, Google, Yahoo, technorati and de.licio.us.

www.millsandboon.co.uk